What They Didn't Know | Adir E. Golan

What They Didn't Know / Adir E. Golan

Contact: adiregolan@outlook.com
ISBN 978-1977627285

What They Didn't Know

Adir E. Golan

This book is dedicated to my parents for helping me achieve my goal and for always believing in me, and to my brother and sisters, nephews and nieces, for putting up with all my…

Thank you, Mom, for helping Michael discover his ancestors' history.

Especially, I want to thank God for making this possible.

INTRODUCTION

A chilled breeze softly brushed the bright orange tree leaves. The sun was rising and had barely started to shine. The grass in the field beside the hospital was a deep emerald green that glittered in the yellow sunlight as it slowly crept, covering everything with a thin sheet of light as morning came.

When Jack Sullivan was born, his mother, Sarah, refused to see him. She did not want to bond with her son because she feared that he might not survive. Jack had been born with a weak heart, and the doctors had warned his parents to be prepared for the worst.

Several days after Jack's birth, his father saw that his condition was improving thoroughly. He tried to persuade Sarah to come see the baby, but she still refused. "What if he doesn't make it, Ben?" she said with tears in her eyes. "I wouldn't be able to handle that." She was to remain at the hospital until her condition improved because, while giving birth to Jack, she had almost lost her life.

A few days later, a nurse came to serve Sarah breakfast. "When are you going to see your son?"

"I can't do it," replied Sarah, feeling guilty.

"I understand. Oh, I almost forgot," said the nurse as she handed Sarah a magazine. "For you to pass the time."

"Thank you." She opened the magazine and out fell a photograph of a tiny baby in an incubator crying as if desperate for help. Sarah stared at the photo for a few long, silent moments and couldn't control the tears rolling down her cheeks. She slowly looked up and saw the nurse waiting beside her bed with a wheelchair. "Let's go see your son…"

- CHAPTER ONE -
THE BEGINNING

The school term was almost over. Everyone was looking forward to the holidays. "This project has to be completed and given to me by the first day of next term. If you're late, you get a big fat zero!" Mr. Brown was a teacher who nobody liked. He was too strict and made everything about his lesson boring. Jack thought that if they had to blow up a building for an experiment, the *bang* would be the only thing that could stop a few from snoring.

At last the bell let out its final shriek for the term. The corridors filled with chaos as the students poured out of the classrooms like a hive of angry bees. Jack forced his way through the classroom door and into the raging corridor. While walking to his locker, he began to feel dizzy and hot. He pushed his way to the deserted bathroom, splashed some cool water on his face, and looked into the mirror. He saw a blood-red Jack stare back through his own brown eyes, which were so shiny they looked as though they were made of glass.

What happened next was completely unexpected. Jack felt his temperature rise and clutched his chest as it filled with pain. He dropped to his knees, and everything went black as he felt himself falling into a dark vortex…

The *Mission Impossible* theme could be heard in the distance and seemed to be getting closer and louder. Jack slowly opened his eyes, reached for his cell phone, which lay on the bathroom floor, and answered in a weak voice. "Hello?"

"Jack, it's Mom. Where are you? School finished forty-five minutes ago. You should be home by now."

"Yeah, I'm on my way." Jack got up off the floor. "I'll be there in fifteen minutes."

"Okay, hurry." Sarah hung up.

Jack lifted his bag and hoisted it onto his shoulder. Before he walked out the door, he looked in the mirror again. This time he saw nothing but large black mark that seemed to have been burned onto the silvery glass. Frightened and unsure of what just happened, he hurried through the school's empty corridors and made his way home.

When he arrived, he walked up the path that cut across the mowed lawn, edged by little flowers. His mother had planted the seeds three years ago and took care of them as if they were her children. Jack still couldn't understand this. He climbed up the stairs that led to the white house with a brown-tiled roof that made it look like an enormous scoop of ice cream with chocolate topping.

"What took you so long?" demanded his mother as he opened

the door.

"I just had to finish off some work for the end of term," lied Jack as he stepped in.

"Well, you should have phoned me to let me know."

"It won't happen again."

His mother sighed and then smiled. "You're lucky it's your birthday. I'll turn a blind eye this time."

Jack smiled in appreciation.

Sarah got up. "Come." She waved her arm to indicate that Jack should follow her. He put his bag on the floor and went into the kitchen after his mother.

"Surprise!" His whole family was standing behind a large round chocolate cake on the kitchen table. There were candles burning on its top, and the smell of matches was in the air.

After singing "Happy Birthday" and eating a slice of cake, they all walked into the old-fashioned living room and slouched on the leather couches that surrounded the rectangular coffee table in front of the fireplace. The fire was crackling softly as it burned. Sarah took a small red box out of her pocket. "Here—happy birthday." Jack opened it and found two small keys with plastic grips and a remote. "It's in the garage," said Sarah. He leaped up and hugged both his parents. "*Wow!*" was the only word Jack could use to describe how thankful he was.

"C'mon," said Kyle, Jack's older brother, who looked like he belonged in a rock band with his long hair. When Jack was a little kid he was convinced he'd seen him on TV, playing an electric guitar beside Bon Jovi. Kyle rushed Jack into the garage, and the rest of the family followed.

"Do you want to take her for a spin?" asked Ben.

"Yes he does, Dad," Kyle answered. He was so excited it was as though *he* were getting the car. Jack got into the shiny black Chevrolet and started the engine. It roared loudly, and he felt a jolt of excitement in his stomach—this was *his* car.

"Front seat's mine!" shouted Jack's sister, Jessica, as she ran to the passenger's seat, her long black hair flying behind her. She had fair skin and bright green eyes. "So you like it, huh?" she asked as she got into the car.

"I love it." Jack seemed unable to stop smiling, and his cheeks began to feel slightly sore.

"I'm the oldest. I should get the front seat, you know," said Kyle haughtily, getting into the backseat.

Jessica laughed. "You can sit here on the way back, Kyle."

"All right, I'll let you off the hook this time," he said seriously.

Jack pressed his foot down and drove off. Everything that had happened at school that afternoon and all the unexplained mystery was washed away and forgotten as suddenly as if it had never happened.

Later that evening, the three of them returned home after a long ride and a stop for ice cream (as if the cake weren't enough). Kyle stayed by the car until Jessica got into the house and then turned to Jack. "Hey, man, I still didn't give you a present."

"What are you talking about? Don't worry about it."

"I'm not worried. I've got it right here."

"Oh."

He began to rummage in one pocket and then moved to the

other. "Where's this damn thing? Ah, there it is." He pulled out a thin silver coin, which reflected the white moonlight.

"Thanks." Jack was confused. "What is it?"

"It's a coin." His brother looked concerned. "Are you sure you didn't have too much of that ice cream?"

"You know what I mean."

"I have no idea. I found it in Dad's car when I was nine. I tried to ask him what it was, but he was too busy working so I just kept it. I tried to buy chocolate with it." He laughed a little. "The guy behind the counter told me it's a token, but I don't think it is. Check it out."

Jack took a good look at the coin. It had a star with eight arms embedded in its face and, when he turned it over, he saw the word *xelticus* engraved in its back. The small letters shone brilliantly as the moonlight crept over them, and it seemed for a second as though fire flashed through the narrow carvings on the silver disc. "Xelticus." Jack read the word out loud. "Do you know what it means?" he asked hopefully.

"Nope." Kyle paced toward the front door and stopped just before walking in. "Err…Jack, you coming?"

Jack had been examining the coin. "Yeah, I'll be right there." He glanced at the coin one more time and put it in his pocket. When he pressed the remote to lock the car, the headlights flashed as it beeped, and Jack saw a shadow drift across the lawn and vanish into the darkness. It was accompanied by a faint noise, which sounded like a speeding car, in the distance. He turned around but saw nothing except for the Robinsons' hedge. He figured that it was probably their cat running around the neighborhood again.

Satisfied with this explanation, he walked into the house and shut the door. That's when it all began...

***

Thousands of miles away—surrounded by mountains, in the midst of the forest—lay a shabby old hut. Ivan was the only person who lived in this area. Most people feared going this deep into the forest, which was why Ivan had decided to live here. He wanted to be alone where no one could find him, with no problems or phones—or any electronic appliances, for that matter.

Wild animals could be heard growling in the distance from time to time. Birds were chirping loudly, and the wind blew gently through the fresh air as it rustled the leaves. Ivan was sitting at his table when he was disturbed by a deafening shriek. He quickly got up and hurried to his bookcase, which had hardly any books but was filled with dirt and cobwebs. Gripping it tightly, he pushed it sideways, causing a loud *crack* accompanied by a cloud of dust. Ivan then pulled the bookcase toward him to reveal a small misshapen hole in the wall behind it.

He made his way through it and lit a lamp that dimly illuminated the dark room. He then moved forward to an empty square table that had nothing but an ancient-looking book covered with a thick sheet of dust. Ivan opened the book, and indented in the cover was a thin silver coin with an eight-armed star embedded in its face. The moment he touched it, the shrieking immediately stopped. Ivan froze, deep in thought for a few moments. He shut the book abruptly, blew out the lamp, and rushed out of the hidden room, clutching the book in one hand and returning the bookcase to its original position with the other. His bedroom contained a bed and a wardrobe that appeared to be approximately one hundred years old. As he opened it, the wardrobe creaked loudly. He took out a bag that had been shoved on one of the shelves and filled it with the old book, a few clothes, and a bundle of money from a piled stash at the bottom of the wardrobe. He hoisted the bag over his shoulder and walked out into the woods.

Ivan had only been walking for an hour or so when he was thrown onto his back by a gust of black wind. He quickly got to his feet and looked around him, turning rapidly from one direction to another as fear and tension took over every fiber of his body.

"Hello, Ivan," said a calm voice from behind.

Ivan spun around to face a pale man dressed in black with leather gloves. "You!" he said coldly.

"Yes *me*. Why do you look so surprised?" asked the man with a smirk on his face. "I thought you'd be expecting me by now."

Ivan did not say a word.

"Well, I'd love to stay and chat, but I'm kind of busy, so I'll just take what I came for and I'll be on my merry little way," said the man in a mocking tone. He bent down and reached for Ivan's bag, which had been lying on the ground. Suddenly, he was blasted against the bark of a huge oak tree and fell face-first onto its thick roots, which emerged from the earth. Smoke was rising from his coat. He got up as though nothing had happened. Both Ivan and the bag were gone. "You got away this time," murmured the pale man, an evil look in his eye. "But it won't happen again, so don't count on it."

Somewhere in London, a man named Richard was enjoying dinner with his wife after a long and stressful day at work. A knock on the door interrupted their meal.

"I'll get it." Richard got up and walked to the front door. He looked through the peephole and quickly opened. "Ivan, are you all right?"

Ivan's clothes were torn, and he had cuts and bruises on his face. "Yeah, I'm fine."

"What happened?"

"Thomas tried to—"

"Honey, what's going on?" Richard's wife had just come out of the kitchen.

"Ivan just dropped by," replied Richard.

"Oh, I thought you were in Australia." She was looking at Ivan now. "What happen…"

"Not anymore," Ivan interrupted rudely and turned to Richard. "We need to talk."

"Okay, er…" Richard felt quite uncomfortable because of the way Allison, his wife, had been looking at him. He knew that he would have to apologize for Ivan's behavior. "Why don't we sit down?"

Once the air had been cleared, the three sat in the lounge, and Ivan told Richard all about his encounter with Thomas. Allison was completely confused. "Okay, time out!"

Both Richard and Ivan stopped talking and looked at her.

"What the hell is going on? Who the hell is Thomas?"

"Um—" Richard started.

"*And…*" continued Allison, raising her voice even more and

raising a hand to silence her husband. "What's the big deal about this book!!" She lifted the old thing from the coffee table and held it in front of their faces. Richard and Ivan exchanged a look before explaining the whole truth to Allison.

"Wait a minute," said Allison with an angry smile. "You're saying that you two are trying to stop this Thomas guy from getting the Zelda coin."

"Xelticus." Ivan said the word slowly.

"*Whatever,*" Allison continued without even looking at him. "Because if he does, he will be very powerful and take revenge, which could cause a big war and a lot of people could die." She took a breath. "Is that right?"

"Well…yeah." Richard had given her a brief summary of the whole story and, when he thought about it, it made no sense at all.

"Just one more thing," Allison started. Richard and Ivan both looked at her hopelessly. "Who started this whole mess? I mean, what triggered the coins to make that weird shrieking noise?"

"Well, when a New Blood—which means someone who has just developed their abilities—touches the coin, it reacts and so do all the others," explained Ivan.

"And you don't know who that is, do you?"

"Nope," said Richard, "but we've got to find them."

"How are you going to do that? This person could be halfway around the world!" said Allison shrilly.

"We start looking," replied Ivan simply.

***

Jack was sitting on the couch in the lounge watching TV. He had just finished his chores and had decided to relax; after all, he was on holiday.

"Hey, Jack, can I borrow your car?" Jessica had just come down the stairs.

"Sure Jessy, but if anything happens to it…" said Jack, smiling.

"If anything happens to it, you've got insurance." Jessica walked out the door.

He only watched TV for forty-five minutes or so and then started to play the guitar. After that, he drove to the Greensville Pool, and by the time he finished swimming, the crimson sun was glittering on the calm water's face.

"Oh, there you are," said Kyle when Jack walked in through the front door. "I was just about to order pizza. Do you want me to get some for you too?"

"Yeah, thanks. I'm just going to shower. I'll be downstairs in ten minutes."

"Okay." Kyle picked up the receiver and dialed. "Hi, good evening. Thanks. I would like to order two family pizzas, thick crust…"

Jack started walking up the stairs and thought that Kyle must have read his mind. He was so hungry after swimming that eating a family pizza by himself would be quite satisfying. As for Kyle eating a family pizza, well, that was normal.

The sun sank farther, and the sky had a beautiful orange color with a tint of red. Clouds were randomly scattered like fluffy clumps of cotton wool. Jack couldn't fall asleep that night. He lay on his back staring blankly at the ceiling. Something was bothering him, but he didn't know what. It was already past midnight, and that's when he heard it again: the soft sound of a car in the distance, as though the air whispered. Sitting up in bed, Jack flipped the switch on the lamp that stood on the cabinet beside him. He looked around, but all he saw was the messy desk against the wall, the yellow guitar in the corner, and the tall built-in cupboard on the other side of the room. He turned off the lamp and tried to fall asleep.

When morning came, he trudged down the stairs and into the kitchen. His family was sitting around the table eating pancakes for breakfast. "Good morning, everyone."

"Did you sleep last night?" asked Kyle as he drowned his pancakes in maple syrup.

"A little bit."

"Come eat breakfast," demanded his mother, as she did almost every single morning.

Ben got up and kissed Sarah on the cheek. "I'm off to work."

"Bye, honey."

"Bye, kids." He walked out.

"Oh, Jack," said Sarah, "your friend Claire called a few minutes ago."

Jack was busy getting orange juice from the fridge and froze for a second. He'd liked Claire since tenth grade but never said anything about it to anyone besides his best friend, Ethan. He had made him take an oath to keep the secret.

"She wants you to phone her," said Sarah

"Did she leave a number?"

"Yes, it's on the phone."

Jack reached for the phone on the wall beside the fridge.

"What about breakfast?"

"In a minute." He pulled the yellow Post-it off the phone and dialed.

"Hello," said a deep voice. Jack assumed that it belonged to Claire's father.

"Hi, it's Jack. Can I please speak to Claire?"

"Hold on."

"Hi," said Claire.

"How's your holiday so far?"

"Great. We just came back from my uncle's beach house yesterday. What about you?" she asked.

"Nothing much." He felt a little nervous. "So er…my mom told me you called this morning."

"Yeah, I called about that science project Mr. Brown gave us for next term."

Jack had completely forgotten about it.

"I was wondering if you want to do it together."

"Sure," said Jack without hesitating. "When do you want to start?"

"How about today, say one o'clock at my place?"

"All right. I'll be there. Bye." He had an odd feeling in his gut.

"Be where?" asked his mother.

"I'm going over to Claire's to do a project for school."

Kyle gave Jack a thumbs up when neither Jessica nor Sarah was looking. Jack laughed, sat down, and ate breakfast with his family.

After breakfast, Jack ran upstairs to get his schoolbag and, as he rushed back down, he snatched the car keys from the wooden bowl on top of the chest of drawers in the lounge.

"Be home by eight o'clock!" Sarah called out before he disappeared out the front door.

"Okay," he replied over his shoulder as he closed the door behind him.

When he arrived at Claire's home, he grabbed his bag from the passenger's seat and walked across the colorful stone path that led to the front door. He rang the bell and waited. Claire's father opened it, clutching a newspaper in his hand. His eyes seemed to be glued to the front page. Finally, he looked up, staring above the frames of his plain, rectangular glasses.

"Can I help you?" he asked, sounding upset by the fact that he had been disturbed. Jack could imagine him sitting by a small square table with a cup of coffee, the paper and a frosted doughnut in his hands.

"Hi, I'm Jack. I'm here to do a project for school with Claire."

"Hold on." Mr. Dawson shut the door in his face abruptly.

Jack heard him calling out to Claire and confirming that "the Jack kid" at the front door was supposed to arrive. The front door then reopened.

"Come on in."

"Thanks," said Jack politely as he entered.

"Claire's down the hall in the lounge." He indicated the direction with a finger. He then returned to reading the front page attentively, lifting a mug off the coffee table and replacing it with his feet as he settled back in his Lazy Boy.

Jack walked to the dining room slowly, looking at the framed pictures hanging on the corridor walls. There was a photograph of Claire's parents at their wedding. Her mother looked like an old-fashioned version of Claire with slightly stronger features, and her father was a lot younger. But he looked quite similar to his present self, sitting in the lounge, other than the hair that used to cover the top of his head a few years back. The frames were filled with memories of Claire and her parents at picnics and theme parks. A little Claire sitting behind a pink cake, blowing out five candles.

Claire was sitting hunched over the table scribbling notes when Jack walked into the dining room. It felt to him as though his heart wanted to break free of the cage it had been imprisoned in for eighteen years.

"Hi," said Claire sweetly. The table was halfway covered with papers full of small writing and diagrams, Claire's laptop sat ready for duty at her side.

"Hi, what's up?" Jack set his bag on the floor and sat in one of the cushioned chairs surrounding the table.

"I'm just preparing a few summaries." She lowered the pen and looked up. Her striking blue eyes glittered in the bright light produced by the chandelier that hung from the ceiling, her blonde hair resting beside her vivid face.

She's beautiful, Jack thought.

"Okay, here's what we've got to do." Claire handed Jack a pile of papers and began to explain. The two sat buried in work until dark.

"That's it," said Claire, satisfied, when they finally finished. "Now we've just got to print it out, and we're done."

"All right, I'll take care of that."

"Would you like to stay for dinner?" offered Claire. The two had cleared the table to reveal an old-fashioned mahogany surface.

Jack glanced at his watch. "Thanks, but I have to be back at home in about ten minutes."

"Oh, sure."

"Hey, um…are you…doing anything else during the holidays?"

"Well, I'm not going to the coast again, if that's what you mean." Claire smiled.

"Yeah," replied Jack promptly. "Do you want to…" The words seemed to be resisting leaving his mouth. "Do something, you know, get a cup of coffee or whatever?" He felt like a weight had been lifted off his chest when Claire responded.

"Yeah, sure." Claire giggled. "I'd love to. Just give me a call."

"I will." Jack felt confidence suddenly grow within him.

The two of them walked to the kitchen, where Claire introduced Jack to her mother, who was busy preparing dinner. She too invited Jack to stay for dinner.

"Maybe another time," she said kindly when Jack explained that he had to go. They reached the front door, and he saw Mr. Dawson still slouching on the couch. Only now he was watching TV.

"Thank you for having me, sir," said Jack before walking out.

"No problem." He forced a smile, which faded almost instantly, and turned his eyes back to the glowing screen.

"Good night," said Jack as he stepped into the cold breeze.

"Bye." Claire smiled and closed the door.

While walking to his car, he could hear the Dawsons. "Claire, tell your father to help you set the table," Mrs. Dawson's voice called out from the kitchen.

"I'll try," replied Claire.

"My show's finishing in five minutes!" whined Mr. Dawson.

Jack got into the driver's seat—it was still hard to believe it was *his* driver's seat—and started the engine. Turning on the radio all he heard was static on every station and it seemed odd to him that the controls were as cold as ice. For that matter, the whole car felt a lot cooler than it was outside. *That's weird.* He began to drive and listened to the engine's song instead.

Jack got home and, before he stepped in, he looked behind him. A nagging feeling lingered, as though he was being watched and followed from the moment he'd left Claire's house. That was when he noticed something move out of the corner of his eye. Turning in one swift motion Jack saw the leaves rustle in the neighbor's bushy hedge. It was undoubtedly large enough to hide a fully grown person.

Slowly, Jack walked toward it, letting curiosity overcome rationality. The leaves still rustled restlessly. He stepped in front of the dark green hedge, hesitated, and then threw his arm forward.

As soon as he touched the hedge, something sprang out. Backing up with a frantic step, he tripped as his heel got caught in a wide crack in the tar driveway. Jack found himself lying flat on his back. A pair of big yellow eyes with slits for pupils was staring at him.

The creature breathed softly and scraped its furry side on his face. He pushed it away and got to his feet. It purred loudly and circled his ankles, the golden light flooding from the streetlamps washing over the striped, silvery hair that covered its entire body.

"Damn it, Mitsy!" said Jack indignantly. "Back off!" He gently nudged the Robinsons' cat aside with his leg.

Mitsy meowed irritably, as if he had hurt her feelings, and bounced back into the hedge. Jack strode into the house, still a little shaken up.

"Hey, Jack."

Jack was staring at the floor when his sister's voice sounded. He looked up anxiously.

"Are you okay?" Jessica was frowning slightly and grinning with a somewhat puzzled look of concern.

"Er…yeah, fine," replied Jack lightly. "It's just Mitsy lurking around again. She jumped out at me."

"Oh." Jessica laughed. "That cat's always a pain. Come have dinner. Everyone's at the table."

"How did the project go?" Sarah asked while placing the hot roast onto her children's plates. It was like an unspoken rule that the entire family obeyed: *when Mom cooks the food, Mom dishes the food.*

"We finished it."

"Already?" She sounded surprised, impressed, and highly curious all at the same time.

"Yeah, first time in my life I finished an entire project in one day!" said Jack proudly. He wrinkled his forehead. "Except for that one time…in seventh grade. I finished that thing about bugs in about two hours."

"And what did you get for it?" Sarah raised her eyebrows, looking at Jack warningly as she laid the roast in front of him.

"I can't remember. But I definitely scraped a pass—I can tell you that much."

"You better hope you get a good mark on your report at the end of this semester, because if you don't…" She poured some of the steaming dish into her own plate and sat down.

"Jack, trust me," Kyle leaned forward. "Even if you get a D minus, just fake a good report for Mom if you want to see the sun again."

Jack laughed.

"You're making me sound like a witch!" said Sarah.

"Hey, I'm just giving him a useful piece of advice." He leaned back in his chair and smiled proudly. "It's my duty as his older brother."

"Honey, where did you find him?" asked Ben comically.

"It was a 'buy one, get one free' kind of situation."

"Who, Jack?"

"Kyle, pass the salt."

"Only if you say the magic word, Jess."

"Now?"

"Yeah, that's the one." He handed her the salt.

"Thanks."

"There it is!" said Kyle happily. "That's my polite little sister. I've taught you well."

"See, Mom?" said Jack. "He's a good role model."

This made Sarah role her eyes.

"This is delicious, Mom," Kyle was looking over his plate.

"He really does live in his own world," said Ben.

"Huh?" Kyle looked up.

They all laughed.

The five of them enjoyed the meal together as a family. Jessica spoke about how working at a hair salon was the worst part-time job ever. She had dyed a customer's hair pink for being impatient with her. At that point Sarah said, "That's my girl." Kyle announced that his band was going to be playing at the upcoming party at Antonio's. Ben said that nothing interesting had happened at the office, as usual. That was when Kyle got up for second helpings, and Jack compared him to a vacuum cleaner.

"At least I'm not fat," was Kyle's reply. This was true. It seemed as though all the food that he ate turned into muscle.

"What's for dessert?" asked Kyle at the end of the meal.

"Wow, your stomach is like a bottomless void," said Jessica. "Just hope that it doesn't come back and bite you in the ass one day."

"I'm just kidding…I can't eat anything now. I'm full. I think."

"Yeah, he'll wait about five minutes or so," said Jack.

"You know me better than anyone, brother." He gave Jack a heavy pat on the back. "You guys want to listen to our new song?"

Sarah was the first to respond, "Ooh, yeah." She loved hearing the new songs Kyle and his band came up with, always saying it was like the good music was finally returning to the world.

"Let's hear it."

Kyle lifted his guitar from the couch and sat on the back of it, and the rest of them settled in around him and listened. He cleared his throat. "'Can't Give Up' by *Attitude*. We've decided on that name, by the way."

"Nice," said Sarah.

"Here goes."

- CHAPTER TWO -
GRADUATION

The summer holidays had gone by so fast and, for that matter, so had life. It felt like only yesterday when Jack was begging his mother not to leave him alone on his first day at school. (He was surprised that he could remember this quite clearly.) And now, all of a sudden, he was wearing a square, flat hat that resembled a helipad, waiting to be called up to the stage by the school's headmaster, whose hair (what he had left of it) had gone completely white, and receive his graduation certificate.

"Hi, Jack."

He turned around. "Claire, where have you been?"

"I was just talking to my parents." She seemed to be unable to stand still, as though she had drunk ten cups of coffee for breakfast.

Jack asked the rhetorical question. "So…are you nervous?"

"Mm-hm." Claire was biting her lip and glancing at the stage, where the other students were receiving rolled-up sheets of paper and smiling at the camera.

"Chris Austin!" the headmaster called out, and Chris began to push through what was meant to be a straight line of pupils.

"Oh, look!" Claire pointed to the seated crowd clapping their hands. "My uncle's here! He said he probably wouldn't be able to make it. I'm so happy he's here!" she said shrilly, without pausing to take a breath.

"Bart Benson!"

"Hey, Claire," said Jack, still eyeing the rows of proud family members. "Where's your dad?"

"He's over there, wearing the black hat."

"Oh, I didn't recognize him." Jack thought that Mr. Dawson looked like Sherlock Holmes in his outfit. All he needed was a magnifying glass.

"Claire Dawson!"

She hurried to the stage through the sea of blue robes. Jack watched as she took the scroll, smiled at the lens, and stood still for the first time that day.

A few more names were called out and then:

"Jack Sullivan!"

Jack strode toward the stage and climbed the stairs that led to the raised platform. He shook the headmaster's hand as he took the sheet of paper, tied with a red ribbon, and stood still for the photo. He could see Kyle and Jessica clapping cheerfully. His dad was waving at him, and his mother was trying to keep the video camera steady while sniffing and crying. The wide smile on her face spread from ear to ear.

A weary pair of eyes was watching, their master hidden behind a bunch of low bushes. Following the Sullivan family as they got into their cars. Watching the younger boy disappear into the black

Chevrolet. His sister followed. Although it would be easier if the boy were alone, the girl couldn't do much but scream. And there would be no one to hear…

Wait, the eldest son—is that him? It must be. His hair is long. But maybe he will not join the other two…there is still a chance that he will leave with his parents… Damn it! Of course he will go with those two. What was I thinking! What am I supposed to do now? I can't capture the New Blood with his brother nearby. He is too skilled, even dangerous. I must abort the plan and return…

There was a soft *whooshing* sound, the leaves rustled slightly, and the space behind the hedges was vacant once more.

"Mom, Dad, is everything okay?" Jack stuck his head out the window to see why his parents were delayed.

"Yeah, sweetie," replied Sarah, her eyes still glowing with tears of happiness, though they were no longer sliding down her face. "We've got a flat tire; your dad's just got to replace it with the spare one in the trunk."

"I'll come help." He opened the door and was about to step out when…

"No, no—you kids go ahead. We'll be there in half an hour," said Ben quickly.

"But—"

"Ah…Ah…don't argue with your father." Sarah smiled. "Go on, we'll meet you there."

"All right." Jack got back into the car and pressed his foot down.

"So what does it feel like to have finished school?" asked Jessica eagerly.

"I feel free," replied Jack honestly.

Kyle laughed. "I remember when I graduated," he said happily. "As soon as the last guy got off the stage, when Headmaster Warbeck was about to invite everyone for refreshments, Drake and I blew up a huge firecracker…" He indicated the size with his hands. "behind the stage where no one could see us." He was grinning jovially. "You should have seen the look on his face!" He started laughing again. "He didn't even hesitate—he just screamed our names at the top of his lungs… Yeah, I miss giving that guy trouble. But he always liked me; he knew I was just messing around with him."

"I'm just glad you didn't give the old man a heart attack," said Jessica.

"Come on, I never went that far."

"You know, I can still picture you doing something like that today."

"Of course, what did a wise man once say? Never lose the childlike wonder," he said dreamily. "Besides, I ran into him today just before the whole thing started, and he said that the school has been missing some action since Drake and I left." Kyle seemed to be rather proud.

"Maybe you should go back," suggested Jessica ironically. "I mean, if it's so *important* to you…"

"Yeah… Maybe…" They had a good laugh as the car continued to drag them along the tar road, the engine moaning quietly.

"That's weird," said Jack, looking ahead and slowing down. There was a roadblock, and a bored man wearing an orange vest with glistening yellow stripes was standing in front of the barrier. He was pointing in the direction of the alternative route with one arm, rotating the other in circles.

"I don't see anything wrong with the road," Jack pointed out.

"Maybe there was an accident or something farther down," suggested Jessica.

"Looks like we're going to have to ride the long way," said Kyle. "But it shouldn't be a problem 'cause I'm sure that Jessy's got a *very* interesting story to tell us on the way.

"I remember something," Jack added. "Something happened that Mom didn't want to tell me about. She said that it would be a bad example for me because I was still small."

"What are you talking about?" Jessica narrowed her eyes, and a curious look grew upon her face.

"You know," said Kyle cheerfully. "That one about your graduation. When you punched—"

"Oh, *that* one! Okay, so everyone's excited that we're graduating and…" She spoke as they continued gliding smoothly on the bumpy road.

***

With a whine the doors swung open in a dark and dingy building. A man with long hair, whose face was hidden by a shaggy beard, stormed in. There were about twenty men sitting around a large rectangular table, some of them smoking, others playing cards, and the rest simply slouching, resting their feet on the elevated surface. Almost every single person had a bottle of beer. None of the chairs matched. Half had torn, moth-eaten cushions, and the other half consisted of plastic and rusting steel. "Where's Thomas?" demanded the man in a rough voice, somewhat like that of a dog's bark.

A massive bald man, who looked rather square, pointed up without bothering to turn his head to see who had asked the question.

Thomas was on the top floor of the building in what used to be an office, many years ago, but was now his home. He didn't sleep, and hadn't done so in over twenty-five years, so a bed would be of no use to him. There was only one small window, in the corner of one of the gray walls. Across from the light-colored door with a dull copper handle lay a large mound of canned food, stacked like a pyramid. Other than that, the room was empty aside from a desk and chair, which also faced the entrance.

Thomas was standing behind the desk, gazing at a chess board. He moved the black queen diagonally across the board. "Checkmate." He tipped over the white king. "Yes," he said when there was a knock on the door, but he continued staring at the king. *Rolling in the shame of defeat,* he thought. "It's always best to play the game on your own," said Thomas dreamily. "That way you always know the opponent's next move…and when you know what's coming, you're always prepared and, most importantly, you always win."

He looked up at once. "Although it takes an *awfully* long time just to finish one game. But nothing to lose, huh?" he said nonchalantly, smiling vacantly.

"We have a problem," said the man brusquely as he entered.

"Oh, it's you—I sent you after that kid, didn't I? Yeah… what's your name again?" He snapped his fingers repeatedly then, without waiting for an answer, said, "You look like a Brian. Let's call you Brian, what do you say?" He paused for an instant then said, "What's the problem?"

"I didn't manage to get what we need."

"What!?" There was a loud bang as Thomas hit the desk hard with both hands. "I told you not to return empty handed!" he said through gritted teeth, leaning forward. "What the *hell* didn't you understand about that!?"

"His brother was with him!" said Brian firmly.

"Oh, I forgot about that." He relented slightly and stood up straight. There was silence while Thomas stared into space, and then he broke it. "Then we wait until he is alone."

Brian was still standing at the entrance. He nodded his head once and shuffled out of the room, shutting the door behind him.

Thomas looked back at the chessboard. He lifted the defeated king and held it tightly between his thumb and forefinger. A soft sizzling sounded from the white plastic as it steadily grew colder. Then a narrow crack crept across it like a spider and quickly spread into a web. Thomas crushed the frozen king to small fragments that trickled to the floor like sea salt.

***

"I can't believe you did that!" Jack was on the verge of laughter. "You *punched* her!" He was thoroughly amused at his sister's graduation reminiscence.

"I went and apologized to her later that day," said Jessica meekly.

"What did she say?"

"She accepted my apology."

"Is that how you became friends?"

"Yep," she said happily.

When they arrived at the restaurant, they put two of the tables together and added a chair in order for the whole family to be able to sit comfortably when their parents got there. The table cloths resembled red and white checkerboards, and the rest of the place matched, with the usual Italian-style colors, shining immaculately.

A waitress came to their table when they settled down. "Would you like to order?"

"Not yet, thanks. We're going to wait for our parents," answered Kyle.

"All right, I'll be back then." She smiled and walked behind the counter into the kitchen.

Sarah and Ben turned up, and the Sullivan family spent the rest of the afternoon enjoying the day out with each other, reminiscing, and telling stories (mostly of high school), all the way back to the year 1977.

***

Jack was standing outside in the garden. He had just stepped out of his new car, which was a birthday gift from his parents. He was the only one there, examining a thin silver coin that glinted in the white light. Something was etched upon it but, for some reason, he could not read the faint carvings. His brother, Kyle, had given it to him, for his birthday, only a few seconds ago, and yet he was no longer there.

Whoooosh.

Jack spun around on the balls of his feet just in time to glimpse a shadow creeping into the darkness of the neighbors' hedge. It stretched from one edge of the world to the other and rose so far up that it reached the calm white rivers that illuminated the violet sky. He slowly paced forward, extending his arm as he drew closer. A blinding flash of light emerged through the leaves as Jack pushed them aside with immense curiosity. He shut his eyes instinctively and felt a cold breeze brush his face…he was on the other side now…on a vast cliff where all he could see when he looked down was thick mist, stirring tranquilly…it was all around. Jack moved through the heavy yet cool air…there was a figure not far from him…he wondered who it was… As he edged nearer, he saw something familiar about this person…she had long blonde hair that draped down her slender shoulders…

"Claire."

She remained motionless.

Jack moved closer. "Claire?" She continued to stand still nonetheless. "It's me, Jack." He put his hand on her shoulder and… she turned instantaneously…but she was different…her hair was as black as charcoal and her face…it was…different.

"Who are you!?" demanded Jack, backing away, staring at the girl in shock.

"You have to be careful," she said anxiously. She was about the same age as he was.

"What?" demanded Jack in bewilderment. "I don't understand. What's going on?"

"Don't let them get it!" She was extremely apprehensive. "No matter what happens, you must protect it at any cost!" The mist grew thicker rapidly…the girl's lips were moving but no sound came out…the wind was too strong…

"What must I protect?" yelled Jack. As though under water he began to float, at the bottom of a cold ocean…he couldn't see her anymore…the fog was too solid… "WAIT!" he yelled, but he could not hear himself anymore…everything slowly turned black…

"Jack!" His name trailed to him from a distance.

Whose voice was that?

"Jack, wake up!" said his mother firmly. "It's just a dream."

He opened his eyes and saw his mother, his father, and Jessica standing over him. They parted like the Red Sea as he sat up in his bed. His shirt was sticking to his back, the air feeling chilled as a result of the sweat that covered his body. "What happened?" He wanted to know what it was that had woken up the rest of the family. Almost the entire dream had slipped away by now. All he could remember were bits and pieces; the details were fading quickly.

"You were shouting," explained Sarah.

"What did I say?"

"We couldn't understand anything you said."

He looked at Jessica hopefully.

"All I heard was…" She made a noise trying to imitate what Jack sounded like, and it made him laugh.

"What's goin' on?" Kyle had just entered Jack's room, yawning widely. His eyes were half closed, and he had a tired, suspicious look on his face.

"Oh, nothing, Jack just had a nightmare," Jessica said.

Kyle looked at his brother, extremely perplexed. "What?"

"I was screaming and I woke everyone up. Didn't you hear me?"

"No. That didn't wake me up," he said wearily, rubbing his eyes.

"What *did*?" asked Ben.

"Jessy," he said simply, still swaying slightly from side to side. "She came into my room and pushed me off my bed."

The attention now focused on Jessica. Everyone seemed to be fully awake now, apart from Kyle. She shrugged and said, "I was half asleep. I thought it was him yelling, and he wouldn't wake up when I called him, so…"

***

That night Jack couldn't fall asleep again. He lay on his back staring at the blank ceiling above, and it didn't seem very long before sunlight filtered through the plain curtains. Jack leaped to his feet and drew back the curtains, letting the light flood the room. The dream continuously played in his head like a film, at least what he could remember. It had felt so real at the time, like all other dreams, but this time it was different. This dream seemed to mean something. Jack had never met that girl in his life. (He could hardly recall what she looked like by now.) But surely he'd seen her face somewhere in the past, maybe on TV or in a magazine. And there was one thing he was certain about: she was not fictional. He had no explanation for how he knew this yet but, somehow, he could tell that she was real even though the situation was not.

But, there must be a rational explanation, he thought, trying to forget about the incident. Yet her voice still rang in his ears: *You have to protect it*. What was he to protect? What could be so important that it was worth any cost? From whom did he need to protect this mystery object?

All these questions floated around in Jack's head like pieces of a jigsaw puzzle that made no sense at all yet still had to fit together to form a clear image. He paid so much attention to this because he deemed it impossible to dream up something like this out of the blue. It had to mean something…but what?

***

"Good morning," said Sarah coming into the kitchen. She seemed surprised to see her son already sitting at the table so early. "How did you sleep last night?"

"I couldn't fall asleep after that dream I had," replied Jack.

"Yeah, what *did* you dream about? Don't you remember anything at all?" she asked while rummaging in the fridge.

"It was…nothing," Jack endeavored to avoid the question, but that never worked with his mother.

Sarah looked at him inquisitively.

"I was standing on a huge cliff, and there was mist all over…"

"Good morning," said Jessica contentedly, entering the kitchen.

"Morning. I gotta go to the bathroom," Jack said, seizing the opportunity to elude his mother's question. He would rather keep this peculiar dream to himself. He wanted to get to the bottom of it without having to explain why he was convinced that it meant something. Jack was not sure how he would answer this riddle, but he knew that he would find a way.

"I'm off to work. Have a nice day, kids." Sarah got up from the table after finishing her breakfast hastily.

"Mom!" said Jessica shrilly when she realized that her mother was just about to walk out the door. She hurried after her. "You said you'd drop me off at work, remember? I just got the new job, and I can't be late on my first day."

"Okay, come on. Let's go!" She turned to Jack. "Finish your chores before you go anywhere."

"I'm already finished."

"How?"

"Didn't sleep, remember?"

"Good for you. Jessy, come on. Let's go!"

"I'm eating in your car. I'm not finished with my breakfast yet."

"Fine, eat on the way—but just this once. I don't want the car to get dirty."

"I'll be careful."

"Hurry up!" said Sarah impatiently. "I have a meeting in twenty minutes!"

Jessica snatched her plate and purse from the table and followed her mother obediently.

"Bye," said Jack as the two disappeared through the door hastily, replying at the same time, "Bye, have a nice day!"

***

The bell chimed about two hours after his mother and sister left for work.

"Hey, man, what's up!" Jack's best friend, Ethan, was standing on the front step.

"Good. What are you doing here so early?" asked Jack.

"It's not early—the time is ten o'clock."

"You always sleep until midday during holidays. What

happened?"

Ethan walked in and slumped on the couch. "A whole bunch of us are going to paintball, and we could use another player. You comin', right?"

"I can't. I've got plans."

"What are you doing?" asked Ethan. He had been Jack's best friend since primary school and knew that Jack hardly ever had plans.

"I'm going to get a cup of coffee with Claire," said Jack simply.

"Claire you had a crush on since tenth grade?" Ethan said smiling, looking eager.

"*Crush* on her... what are you, nine?," said Jack firmly.

Ethan burst into laughter. "All right, whatever you say. I just want you to know that I'm really proud of you, man," he said lightheartedly. "You finally mustered up the guts to do something about it!"

Jack grimaced with a false smile.

"So I'm gonna take off." Ethan stood up and cut across the living room to the doorway. "Everybody's meeting up in the arena in about fifteen minutes." He walked out and then turned to face Jack. "But I still can't believe that it took you three years—*three years!*" He chortled again.

"I don't want this to be a headline in tomorrow's paper, so just try and keep your mouth shut, okay?"

"I'll do my best." Ethan began to walk away. "But I can't promise anything."

"Hey!" Jack called out in an intimidating tone.

"Fine…I'll be quiet."

"Yeah, you do that," said Jack as he closed the door.

At last, the time had come. Jack got into his car and went to pick up Claire. Parking outside her house he stayed seated behind the steering wheel. After a couple of minutes, he took a deep breath and sighed and stepped outside, progressing along the winding stone path leading to the pale, creviced wooden door. He lifted a fist and knocked steadily.

"Who's there?" Jack recognized Mrs. Dawson's voice, sounding impatient.

"It's Jack… I'm here to pick up Claire," he explained.

"Hold on. Claire!"

"I'm coming." A few moments later, the door whined open and there she stood.

All of a sudden, Jack saw her in a completely different way. Before, he had liked her a lot. But now there were feelings that he could not elucidate. It was the first time he'd ever felt this way about a girl.

"Hi," she said amiably.

Jack's speech control was temporarily impaired, but he quickly recovered and said, "Wow, you look great."

Claire smiled, and her cheeks turned a slightly crimson shade as she treaded slowly toward the car.

"Have fun, kids." Mrs. Dawson was standing at the entrance.

"Okay," said Claire.

"Jack, drive safely," said Mrs. Dawson kindly.

"I will."

Mr. Dawson came too, arms folded. "I want you back here before it starts to get dark—do you understand?" He was staring at Jack through narrow eyes.

"Of course," said Jack quickly. "You can count on it, sir."

"Good…as long as we're clear on that."

"Bye, Mom. Bye, Dad," Claire said before an awkward silence kicked in, and it was bound to. Her mother was looking at her proudly. Her father, on the other hand, was eyeing Jack apprehensively. She began to head toward the car once again.

"Bye." Jack turned gracefully and hurried past Claire to open the door for her.

"Thanks," she said, beaming, as she got in. Jack closed the door after her and went to the driver's seat. He started the engine and, out of the corner of his eye, saw Mrs. Dawson waving excitedly at her daughter. Mr. Dawson was standing still. Jack could not see him clearly, yet he knew that he was still staring at him. Jack set off before Claire's father burned a hole in the side of his head just by looking at it so intensely.

"Forgive my parents, this is my first official date, so…" said Claire once they were both inside.

"Yeah me too."

"Really?" she said, shrugging, "I always assumed otherwise."

"Huh…"

"I don't like him," Mr. Dawson said grumpily as he watched the black Chevrolet drift away.

His wife sighed and rolled her eyes. "Here we go again," she said impatiently.

"Are you happy to be finished with school?" Claire asked Jack when they were halfway across the small bridge that rose over the shallow stream that flowed calmly. Old wooden planks and logs creaking as the water lapped not far below their feet.

"Rhetorical question right? It's one of the best things that ever happened to me," replied Jack, delighted. "Don't get me wrong—I enjoyed it while it lasted, but now that it's finished you can…live life, you know?"

Claire smiled while gazing at the tall tree tops that mantled the lush landscape around them. Every time she smiled, Jack felt that odd sensation in his gut—the same one he'd experienced earlier when he went to pick her up—he was beginning to get used to it. "What about you?" he asked.

"It's fun," said Claire wide eyed. "I'm going to work at a part-time job as a waitress at Antonio's until I start studying at university."

"Cool. What are you going to study?"

"Medicine."

"You would make a great doctor."

She laughed again. "How do you know?"

"Because ever since I've known you, when you wanted something you've always gotten it—one way or another."

"What do you want to do?" she asked, amused.

"That is a very good question. I should have an answer by now but I have no idea."

"It's a start."

The two of them gazed into the distance. Claire's cell phone rang and broke the tranquil silence.

"Hello? Yeah. Okay. Bye." She hung up and straightened up, ready to go.

"What's up?" asked Jack, hoping not to get the answer that he did.

"Sorry, I have to get home early. We're going to my Aunt Nina's, and we want to be in time for dinner—it's her anniversary," though she did seem disappointed, which Jack took to be a good sign.

Jack was relieved to know that she was enjoying herself as much as he was. "Come on, I'll drop you off."

Once they arrived at Claire's house, she did not get out of the car immediately. "Thanks, I had a lot of fun," she said coyly.

"Me too."

They looked at each other, and there was a silence so loud it could almost be heard. Jack looked into her blue eyes, which sparkled like diamonds in the setting sun's tranquil radiance, and she stared back. They both began to move forward tentatively. Jack felt as though his heart and lungs had stopped functioning for a moment. Suddenly, the front door of the house swung open, and they both moved back like a pair of magnets repelling each other. Claire opened the car door, said "Bye," and hurried into her home. Her father was standing on the doorstep as still as a statue, glaring. Jack turned his head to look straight ahead as he ignited the engine without further delay, afraid to make eye contact because he might turn to stone.

- CHAPTER THREE -
FLIGHT NO FIGHT

Allison and Richard were packing their things into two large suitcases that lay open on their bed.

"Richard," said Allison.

"Yeah."

"How exactly does Ivan plan on finding this person?"

"I have no idea," replied Richard honestly. "But I'm sure he's got a plan." He leaned on the fat, stubborn suitcase and closed the zipper. "All done!"

"By the way," Allison was on her knees rummaging in the bottom of their wardrobe. She stood. "Where are we going?"

"America."

"Why there?" She added something to the suitcase, which was already too full.

"Well, Thomas is—"

"Honey, can you help me with the suitcase?"

"Sure. Thomas lives there, and he has definitely found the New Blood person by now. If this person weren't in America, Thomas wouldn't be there." The case finally closed when he pressed on it with his elbow. "He's the kind of person who doesn't waste time. And I bet he's got one of his people keeping an eye on the target as we speak."

"One of his people?" said Allison, perplexed.

"His got…er…followers. He has convinced anyone will listen to join him. You know, people who have powers. Anyone that's been hurt in some way and wants to get back something they lost…anyone who is angry at the world—you know what I mean?"

"Yeah."

"Are you two ready?" Ivan was standing at the entrance to their bedroom.

"Where did *you* come from?" demanded Allison derisively.

"I just got here."

"Don't you knock?" a sarcastic smile flashed across her face.

"The door was unlocked so I let myself in. The flight leaves in an hour, and we should really get going now."

***

The gargantuan metallic bird howled loudly as it glided back to earth, only on different soil this time.

"Richard, Allison…" Ivan turned in his seat to face them. "When we get off the plane, my friend Lenny is waiting outside the airport with his cab. I've already arranged everything with him. He's going to give you a ride to the hotel. I booked room 278 for you two, and I'm in 280."

"Right next to us—isn't that great," murmured Allison, dejected.

Ivan did not hear her. "I'll meet you there tonight. I just need to take care of a few things."

"What do you need to take care of?" asked Allison suspiciously. Richard looked at her and smiled. Apparently amused at how she enjoyed picking on Ivan, who didn't care at all.

"Making sure that Thomas doesn't know exactly where we are."

Allison did not find this a satisfying answer. Nevertheless, she discontinued arguing with Ivan. Until she was left alone with her husband she remained silent. They began to walk toward the exit of the airport, and she said, "I have a bad feeling about this."

"What are you talking about?"

"This whole thing of us going alone in a cab in a country we hardly know anymore. I mean, it's been years since we lived here. And Ivan…he's…"

"You know we can trust Ivan, I know he is not your best friend, but still—it's Ivan."

"I know. I trust him. But he's acting very odd. He doesn't look very confident."

"Come on, Ivan is always weird," said Richard humorously, but Allison was not amused. "Look," he explained calmly. "I've known the guy since high school. He's my best friend."

"It just… seems like he's hiding something."

"He's worried. We can trust him; I'm one hundred percent sure." He saw Allison's expression. "Okay?" he added hopefully.

She sighed. "Okay." They stepped outside of the airport into the blustery environment. There were more than a half a dozen cabs parked by the pavement, but only one of the drivers was leaning on his mud-sprayed yellow car, waiting. He looked like he had just come back from Hawaii, wearing white shorts, a T-shirt bearing large flowers, sunglasses with purple shades, and a beret.

"There, that's probably him." Richard jerked his head in his direction. "Excuse me."

The man was talking on his phone and noticed the couple standing in front of him.

"Can I help you?" His moustache vibrated when he spoke.

"Are you Lenny?" asked Richard hopefully.

"Yes." Lenny frowned. "Ah!" he said so loudly and suddenly that Richard and Allison both recoiled. Lenny's frown disappeared, and his face glowed with a wide smile that revealed his shiny golden tooth surrounded by yellow smoke-stained teeth. "You're Ivan's friends! Ritchie and Alice, right?" he said enthusiastically in a Spanish accent.

"Yes." They both nodded simultaneously. They did not want to correct Lenny; they wanted to speak to him as little as possible. Not because he was unfriendly—he was very friendly and gave the impression of being a good-natured person—but each time he spoke it was like a sprinkler splashing in their faces.

Lenny turned on the radio once they had started driving. "I love this song!" he exclaimed as he raised the volume and began to sing along. "You guys are gonna love it here in America." Lenny was shouting in order to be heard above the loud music. "Ivan told me you are from London, but I don't hear the accent."

"We used to live here—we only moved to London a couple of years ago," bellowed Richard.

"Ah! Then I bet you're already having fun, eh?"

"You bet," yelled Allison sardonically exchanging a private look with her husband.

After fifteen minutes or so, the driver turned off the radio Looking worried. Incessantly glancing at the rearview mirror.

"Lenny? Something wrong?" Richard was concerned.

"See that car on our tail?"

Richard turned in his seat and saw a black Jeep with tinted windows and blank license plates. "What about it, besides the license plates? I mean…it could be a new car." But even he didn't believe this as he said it, growing anxious by the second.

"I think he's following us."

"*Why?*" asked Allison worriedly.

"'Cause I've seen him there since we left the airport"

Allison did not like what she was hearing at all. "Well, what are we going to do!?" she demanded shrilly.

"I'm gonna take us down to the police station." Lenny was still glancing at the mirror.

"How far is it?" asked Richard in a confident tone.

"There's one nearby. Just a bit over five minutes from here."

The black vehicle was edging nearer.

"Oh my God—STOP THE CAR!" Allison cried.

Lenny looked ahead and hit the brakes immediately when he saw someone standing in front of them in the middle of the road. He stuck his head out of the window. "Hey, man! What the hell are you doing?" he yelled at the figure dressed in black. "If you don't move, I'm driving over you!"

The man walked up to the window. "Get out of the car," he said coldly and serenely. He wore sunglasses and had a horribly serious look on his face.

Lenny locked the doors. "Sorry, I'm really busy, maybe another time, I gotta go," he uttered nervously, rolling up the window. "Now if you'll excuse me—"

He was about to drive away but, before he could, the muscular bald man forced his hand through the window, unlocked the door, and viciously pulled Lenny out into the road.

They were now stuck out there with a dense forest to the right and a steep slope to the left. And it was especially odd that there was not another soul in sight. "Back off!" Lenny tried to fight back but got punched hard in the face, leaving him to lay helpless on the gritty tar with a bleeding lip.

The doors of the Jeep slid open, and four other men—bearing the same attire as the assailant who had attacked the driver: a black coat, black gloves and a shirt and trousers to match—stepped out. Richard and Allison were sitting in the backseat of the taxi as silent as fish.

"Get them out," the square-built man ordered the others. Two of them hauled Richard and his wife out, but they weren't as rough as expected.

"Richard, I'm scared," murmured Allison. "Can't you get us out of this—just do your thing?"

"I'd rather not."

"*What?*" she hissed anxiously.

"These guys are working for Thomas," he elucidated.

"So?" Their hands were cuffed behind their backs, and they were being led to the car. "You can take on half a dozen thugs!"

"They won't hurt us, but we will end up getting hurt if we try anything. They can...do *things* as well."

"Max!"

The man who seemed to be in charge turned to face the one who had called him.

"What about the taxi, and this guy." He nudged Lenny in the ribs with his foot, causing him to grunt. The driver still appeared terrified, staring apprehensively from one end of the conversation to the other.

"Put him in the back with their stuff. I'll take care of the taxi."

The other man nodded once and followed the instructions.

Meanwhile, Max got into the yellow cab and drove forward. As soon as he picked up some speed, he turned the steering wheel all the way to the left, toward the slope. The car swerved sideways sharply and rolled away from the road, windows shattering as it smashed into the side of the slope. Allison watched in amazement and so did Lenny, just before he was shoved in the back with the suitcases. Richard was not surprised. The shards of glass and metal could be heard as they splintered in the air. And then, just before reaching the bottom of the slope, the car exploded into a huge mushroom inferno, emitting thick, black smoke that slowly rose into the sky.

Allison's mouth was still open. The men in black were laughing.

"Get in!" one of them snapped at Allison.

Richard turned and, without warning, gave him a solid punch square in the face, and Allison gasped. The man fell to the ground. "Don't talk to her like that," said Richard sternly.

The other got back to his feet with a red mark on his flat face. He was bleeding from his nose and—while his fist was in midair to hit Richard, who was ready to fight despite what he'd said earlier—

he was stopped and hurled back.

"What did Thomas tell you?" asked Max indignantly. "Now go—drive."

The man looked at Max then at Richard. He smirked and walked away. Allison was stunned. Max had just been in an explosion, and now he was standing right there, preventing her husband from being hurt. For some reason, these were the orders Thomas had given out. None of this made sense, and then she remembered being told that they too were…different.

"Get inside," Max said abruptly and followed.

"Richard…" Allison had tears in her eyes. "What's happening? What are we going to do?"

"Quiet," interrupted Max without so much as looking at them.

***

Ivan arrived at The Madison Hotel that evening. After checking in, he climbed up the stairs and knocked on the door across the hall from his room. Richard and Allison should have arrived by now. "Anybody home?" He pounded again, but there was no reply and the door was locked. Grunting in frustration he made his way back down to the lobby.

"Excuse me."

"Yes sir, how can I help you?" asked the woman standing behind the counter, a fake smile spread across her cheeks.

"Did a couple check in this afternoon, in room 278?"

"I'm sorry, it's the hotel's policy that all information about our guests remains classified," she said frostily, still pretending to be cheerful about what she obviously hated doing.

"Please, this is really important. They were supposed to be here this afternoon, under the name Brant."

"I'm sorry, there's nothing I can do for you, sir."

"I'll even show you that—"

"Sir!" she said impatiently. "If you don't leave *right* now, I'm going to have to call security."

Ivan walked away without saying another word. He *had* to find out if his friends had arrived at the hotel or not, and he could not attract attention—at least not to himself.

A couple with two kids came into the lobby sometime after Ivan had left. While they were standing at the counter waiting for their keys, the double doors to the kitchen flung open. Waiters and chefs were running through them as the fire began to spread into the dining area and the foyer began to fill with smoke. The family that had just entered had already left, and people coming down the stairs, to see why there was so much screaming, began to panic as well.

The secretary ran to the other side of the lobby to hit the emergency button for the fire alarm, because it had not been set off automatically like it should have been. While she was doing so, Ivan came running down the stairs with his bag on his back and hurried to the computer that stood unattended on the reception desk. Unnoticed, consequent to the disarray, he typed in the name "Brant" and saw that Richard and Allison had not arrived at the hotel that afternoon. Knowing that this meant trouble, there was no time to waste, especially if he did not want anyone to get hurt.

Ivan sprinted toward the raging flames and right into them. Moments later, the fire began to get sucked back into the kitchen. It got smaller and smaller and looked like a tiny twister made of bright yellow flames.

This "twister" slowly began to die as it lost oxygen and faded away. When it was finally gone, all that remained was smoke. Ivan stood there, looking around him, making sure that the fire was completely gone. Then he swiftly got out of the hotel unnoticed.

***

Richard and Allison were locked in the office where Thomas lived. They had been put in there and told that they would wait until he arrived. Finally, after they had spent a couple of hours sitting on painfully uncomfortable steel chairs, the door opened and Thomas glided in, or so it appeared.

He was smiling. Coldly.

"What do you want from us?" asked Richard.

"Oh, come on! Not even a *hello* after all these years? I'm hurt." He always acted in this unusual manner. Slouching in the chair behind his desk he lifted his feet on the metallic surface of the table. "Why are you here?"

"Why are *we* here?" repeated Richard indignantly. "You sent your little henchmen after us!" He glared at him.

"C'mon, Richard, you're not stupid." Thomas's face suddenly grew serious. "You know exactly what I mean. Don't play dumb."

Richard did not say a word.

"Why did you come back from London? You don't have

anything here anymore. You lost your job; you were on the verge of losing your house. And, if I recall correctly, the deal was: you get the hell out of here and never come back." He dragged his feet off the table and sat forward in his chair.

"There was no deal, Thomas!" Richard bellowed. "You took everything away from us until we were forced to leave!"

"And I gave it all back when you did," said Thomas simply.

"Yeah, so no one would get in the way of your little mission. You never wanted to listen to anything any of us had to say—"

"I still don't," he interrupted promptly.

"I don't have time for this." Richard stood up.

"Where do you think you're going? I've got the place surrounded."

"Thomas, you and I both know that it's no problem for me to get us out of here!"

"Us?" Thomas had a puzzled expression on his face. "Oh." He turned to Allison, who had been sitting quietly the entire time. "I'm so sorry, I forgot you were here," he said in a false sympathetic tone. "I'm such a terrible host. Would you like something to drink?"

Allison preferred not to answer the crazy man's question.

"Richard…" Thomas turned again. "How about you?"

Silence.

"No? Nothing? Well, I've got to go. I have a few errands to run." He stood up. "Just make yourselves at home. You can have as much of *that* as you want." He pointed to the large stack of canned food in the corner as he headed for the door. "There's a can opener and a few disposable spoons in the bottom right drawer. But, for some reason, the food's all *really* bitter." He gave Richard a disgruntled look, opened the door, and paused. "Oh, right. It almost slipped my mind to inform you that the New Blood will probably be joining us soon." He smirked. "I hope you don't mind sharing the room." He disappeared though the opening, and the door slammed behind him.

"Can you please explain to me what the hell is going on?" said Allison at once. "What does he want from us!?"

"To use us as bait to get Ivan to come here. Also he wants everyone that can possibly make his life harder to be out of the way."

"How are we going to get out of here?"

Richard walked to the corner of the room, picked up a pile of cans, and carried them to the door, where he dropped them on the floor. "Honey, I've got a plan. Help me move these cans over here."

"Okay," said Allison, completely puzzled, and she started to help. "Why are we doing this?"

"So that we can get out of here."

"Didn't you say earlier that you don't want to do anything because we'll just wind up getting hurt?"

"Yes, I did. But now we can do it without getting hurt 'cause they won't be able to get to us."

"Because we're going to block the door with canned food— isn't that right?" Allison said contemptuously.

"Yep."

They settled the last of the cans in front of the door.

"All right, stand behind me." Richard raised both hands. Allison stood back as he had asked; now she realized what his plan was. He was facing the door, and he narrowed his eyes. His hands glowed red…

On the other side of the door, two of the men in black were standing on either side of the narrow doorposts like obedient sentries.. From within the room a muffled roar echoed. One of the guards twisted the brass handle.

"Arrgh!" He backed away from the copper sphere like a cat from cold water. "Damn it!" The skin on his hand was burned, and when the two looked at the handle again, they watched it smolder bright crimson.

"Call Max!" he ordered his acquaintance. "Hurry up!" He was clutching his scalded hand with the healthy one. There was a *whoosh* and, two seconds later, a mammoth dark figure was looming at the top of the staircase.

"What?" Max demanded through gritted teeth.

The man gestured with his head to the door. Smoke seeped slowly from the thin sliver by the floor.

Max placed the palms of his hands flat on the wooden surface. A faint whistle sounded as it froze and cracked all over. He took a step back and kicked hard. The block of ice smashed into large pieces, which crashed to the floor and shattered to hundreds of minute shards, which sank slowly into the carpet, cold steam rising as they began to melt.

The three of them entered the empty room. A conspicuous rotund hole in the exterior wall let the cold wind rush inside. Ashes were still shimmering on the edges of the cavity, glowing slightly brighter with every breath the air took, molten steel still oozing from the crest of the bulky opening.

Peering outside, Max saw nothing but the black night stretched across the sky like a murky canvas and empty moonlit streets with a few dim streetlamps, scattered, flickering. Most were burned out. Faded pieces of newspapers were gliding in the chilly stream of air. Richard and Allison were gone suffice to say.

CHAPTER FOUR

IN YOUR DREAMS

Again he was standing on the tall cliff surrounded by mist. The rivers in the violet skies were flowing peacefully, just like the last time he had visited this place. But there was no hedge. Jack peered through the white air. He was looking for the girl he had seen here before. During their last encounter she had left him with an ambiguous and unfinished message, and Jack wanted to know what it was that he had to protect. This was not just a dream…he could feel that it was real.

An anxious voice came from behind Jack. "They're going to come for you." He spun around and saw her: the same girl with the black hair. She wore a silver necklace around her neck, holding a key that glinted in the mauve light.

"Who's coming for me?" asked Jack, yearning to receive an answer.

"You must be careful," she warned. "You *have* to protect it!"

Everything was foggy and vague. The rivers high above were raging, and the fierce wind blew harder than ever through the dense air.

"I don't know what I need to protect!" His voice echoed disconcertedly.

"Xelticus," said the girl at once. Her voice sounded as though it came from far away, yet it was so loud. Suddenly, everything was silent. The water stood still, the wind hushed, and darkness began to creep in high up. The girl looked terrified. "I have to go." Her whisper hissed in Jack's ears like a serpent's.

"Wait! Who are you?" Jack was eager to know more but, before he knew it, he was lying awake in bed. Wide eyed, he stared at the small alarm clock that was ticking tediously on his bedside table. It was almost five o'clock, and outside it was still dark. And then he remembered it.

Jack sprang out of bed, opened a drawer, and began to rummage hastily. He then pulled out the silver coin that Kyle had given him on his birthday...

"Xelticus...do you know what it means?"
"No idea..."

The voices resonated in his mind. Jack froze, eyes still wide open. Once again he read the slanted letters on the reverse of the cold object. *"Xelticus."*

***

"That's spooky," confirmed Ethan when Jack drew a breath after telling him about the peculiar dreams and unexplained weirdness that had occurred lately. He still left out the part about the coin and replaced it with the fact that the girl in his dreams 7knew his name. He preferred to be cautious, just in case.

"You think?" Jack said ironically.

"And you definitely don't know this girl?"

"No, I told you she's in my dreams. I've never seen her before."

"Maybe you've seen her in a poster or something like that," suggested Ethan.

"Fine. Maybe I did, but that doesn't explain how she knows my name."

"Look, I know this is *really* weird for you, but I'm sure that there's a rational explanation for this whole thing. I mean, a girl you've never met before coming into your dreams and warning you that people are out to get you is kind of odd." Ethan sighed. "Listen man, I'm sure you've seen this girl's face somewhere. You just don't remember—it's in your subconscious or something…"

"But it was so real," said Jack desperately.

"What dream isn't?" He was lying on the Chinese-style couch, which looked like it came straight from Beijing, staring at the paneled ceiling of his large house.

Jack hated the fact that Ethan was arguing a good point.

"It's reality, and then you wake up and snap out of it," Ethan reasoned. "Someone contacting you through your dreams—that's pretty farfetched, don't you think?"

"Yeah, I know," agreed Jack. "But since my birthday, this is the only dream I've been having."

"You're just dwelling on this one so much that you don't remember the other ones."

Although not satisfied with this explanation, Jack decided to put the matter to rest. Besides, this *did* make the most sense.

"You're paying way too much attention to this. Just let it go, man."

"You're right."

"Great." In one motion, Ethan lifted his head and stood up. "Now that that's been settled... Next week, Sunday night, there's that annual party at Antonio's. They have a band and all that stuff. You know, like last year." He looked at Jack expectantly.

"Yeah, I remember. Kyle's going to play a few songs with the band. What are they called...Void."

Ethan nodded dismissively. "Uh huh, good music, screwed up name. You gonna bring Claire?" He looked at Jack determinedly.

"I'm sure she's going anyway," said Jack absentmindedly.

"I know but..." He paused and looked at Jack with anticipation. "*You* should bring Claire..."

"Oh..."

"There it is," said Ethan resolutely. "You owe me one!"

"You still owe me five bucks."

"Then we're even."

As soon as Jack got home, he went to the phone and called Claire at her home. Her cell phone was still in for repairs. He remembered her telling him about being pushed into the pool by her cousin at the beach house when her cell was in her pocket.

He recognized Mrs. Dawson's voice.

"Hi, it's Jack."

"Hi, Jack. How are you?"

"I'm all right, thanks. How are you?" he asked politely.

"Couldn't be better. You want me to call Claire?"

"Yes, please."

"Claire!"

Jack drew the receiver from his ear when Mrs. Dawson shouted.

"Oh, she's not home, but I'll tell her you called."

The doorbell rang. "Okay, thank you." He put the receiver down and went to open the door. "Is there a…Jack Sullivan here?" asked the jaded deliveryman.

"Yes, that's me."

"I've got a package for you." He handed him a rectangular box and a clipboard. "Please sign here."

Jack hadn't been expecting anything. "Who is it from?" he asked when he saw that the box was blank aside from his own address scribbled on the box untidily.

"No name or address," replied the man, taking back the clipboard. "This sloppy work showed up at the post office this mornin'—*stupid policy*," he murmured.

Wrapped inside the package, with newspaper cuttings, was a small jewelry box and an envelope. Jack opened it and read the short letter that was enclosed. It was scribbled in the same messy writing that was scrawled on the plain box.

Dear New Blood,

I am sorry that I was not able to deliver this to you in person. It is vital that that you keep this key safe and make sure that it remains a secret that you possess it. I don't know your name and I haven't met you before, not formally at least. I know that this is probably very confusing for you, and none of this makes any sense at all. It may even seem childish, but it is more serious than you know.

Everything will become clear in due time. Hoping to meet you soon.

Keep Safe
The girl in your dreams

Jack stared at the letter blankly for several seconds before he realized that he had forgotten something due to his sudden state of shock. He quickly opened the black jewelry box and froze when he saw what was inside. It was the key he had been expecting, but it was not just any key. This was the same key that he had seen around the girl's neck in his dream.

Who was she? How did she know where he lived? Why did she refer to him as "New Blood"? How was she getting into his dreams? Jack's head was swarming with questions, but the one to which he was most keen to find the answer was: *What does this key open?*

There was no way of finding out. For now, all he could do was keep the secret until, in "due time," everything was supposed to make sense. It felt like the right thing to do.

***

The tables at Antonio's had been moved aside to provide space for a dance floor, and they were all occupied.

"Jack, over here." Ethan signaled him and Claire from one of the tables. "I saved you two a seat."

"They really put a lot of work into it this time," said Claire as they sat down.

"Guys, I'd like you to meet Cindy. Cindy, Claire, Jack," Ethan said. "And this is Pete."

"What's up?" Jack shook Pete's hand.

The band played the last note of the song, and the hall filled with cheers. Someone walked up to the stage and spoke to the guitarist walking off of it. He pointed to someone carrying a black electric guitar with green flames spread on its body. The teenager nodded and walked up to Kyle. Kyle patted him hard on the back and ran up the few stairs leading to the top of the stage. Again the crowd applauded enthusiastically. This time, Jack, Claire, and the others at their table clapped and whistled. Kyle waved to them and started the introduction to the next song.

"Claire, do you want a drink?" asked Jack.

"Yeah, I'll have a Coke. Thanks." She smiled. She had started a conversation with Cindy, and they looked as if they had known each other since they were born. Jack made his way through the crowd to the counter to get served.

"Jack, wait up!" Ethan caught up with him. "So how's it goin' man?" he said gleefully.

"Everything's great," replied Jack, glancing at the stage. "Hi, can I please have two Cokes?"

"Make that four," Ethan cut in.

"Four Cokes coming up," responded the waitress happily.

Jack glanced at the stage again.

"What are you looking at?" asked Ethan.

"I'm waiting for the song to finish."

"Why?"

"I want to make a request."

"Oh ho ho! What song?"

"You'll see, Santa." The song ended and Jack hurried across the floor, leaving Ethan to wait for the drinks.

"That's my favorite song!" exclaimed Claire when the instruments began to sound the music. Jack and Ethan arrived at the table with the drinks and set them down.

"May I have this dance?" Jack tried to hide the fact that he was nervous as much as possible; he could *feel* the blood pumping in his veins.

"Yes," she contently said and she took his outstretched hand. They moved to the dance floor, and Kyle caught Jack's eye.

"I think you're going to have to take the lead on this one. I'm not very good at this."

Claire giggled.

They began to dance to the slow song, and Jack felt his heart crushing his ribs once more. The song flowed on…

***

Overall, it had gone quite well. Jack had survived the whole song without stepping on Claire's toes even once. When they arrived at her house after the party, Jack walked with her to the door, and she stopped before she went in. "I had a lot of fun tonight."

"Yeah, me too."

"Thanks for the dance. You weren't *so* terrible."

"We should do it again sometime."

They stared into each other's eyes and slowly moved closer. Jack's heart was racing, and he couldn't remember a time when he had been this nervous in his life. They closed their eyes. They put their hands on each other's arms. They kissed. The wind fell silent, and the grasshoppers hushed as the world fell away for a few moments. An awkward silence followed until Claire said, "Good night."

"Night," Jack replied quickly.

Claire walked inside and Jack got into his car.

While driving home, Jack's mind was occupied only with what had just happened. He felt so different now, thinking about Claire.

All of a sudden, someone appeared in the middle of the road, and Jack stopped the car just before colliding with the person. He looked at the dark figure that stood as still as the night that surrounded them. Jack hooted, but the silhouette did not shift away. It began to move closer to the car, dragging its black coat.

Jack pressed his foot flat on the gas and sped forward, right past it. He looked in the mirror and saw the shadow watching the car drift away. Jack watched the road, and when he glanced at the mirror again, he saw nothing but the black night. But he could hear something. The sound was identical to what he had heard on the night of his birthday and that other night in his room, when he couldn't fall asleep. Only now it was louder than ever. Jack looked sideways to where the sound seemed to be most amplified and saw something through the window that he had never seen anywhere before, something so unreal.

A black wind that stretched as long as the car was blowing beside him. Frost began to creep on the window from the edges of the glass. It grew so cold inside the car that Jack could see his breath when he exhaled. The frost steadily started to spread on the windshield, making it almost impossible to see through it. Jack looked aside again and saw a black current of air. Fear took over every fiber of his being. He could barely see where he was going, but he did not dare stop the car. He tried to activate the wipers, but they were frozen.

"COME ON!" he shouted desperately. Squinting through the hazy window beside him, he saw the wind turn its hollow face on him. It stared at him through blank eyes as pale as ice. There was nothing but a chilling void of white. Jack gasped in terror and, as much as he could, focused on the road ahead. And just when he thought that this was how he was going to die, he saw home. Swerving sharply onto the lawn, he crushed his mother's flowers and the wheels dug up furrows of earth. The tires screeched loudly as he pounded the brakes.

The front door swung open a moment after he came to a halt, and Kyle came rushing out. "JACK!" he yelled apprehensively, sprinting to his brother. "Are you okay!? What happened?"

"I—I don't know," Jack stammered in alarm. The black wind had gone and so had the frost. The wipers were waving violently, and everything seemed to have returned to normal. Jack twisted the plastic knob and put the wipers to rest. Aside from his "crash landing" in the yard, it was as though nothing had happened. "I guess I…lost…lost control of the car." He was shaking violently.

Kyle sighed in relief. "Get inside. Have something to drink. I'll park her for you."

"I can park—"

"Hurry up, before Mom and Dad come home." He raised his eyebrows.

"Thanks."

Jack went into the kitchen and gulped down a full glass of water. As soon as he finished swallowing, his head started spinning, and the empty glass shattered on the floor when he tried to set it down. His chest swelled with blinding pain. Jack thought he was going to pass out just like the last time he had felt this like this; the memory flashed back to him more clearly than ever. Only now his body heat rose to a point at which he could no longer stand the heat. Instinctively, he ripped open his shirt, the buttons tapping silently on the kitchen counter. The attempt to cool off was futile. He choked in horror at the implausible sight burning before his eyes.

The skin on his chest seemed to be dissolving into a fiery crimson. The normal flesh color appeared to have holes that widened so fast, resembling a smoldering plastic bag. Fear took over his every emotion and filled him. Jack's vision blurred, and he saw a hazy spurt of flames. He dropped to his knees and fell unconscious…

***

As he slowly opened his eyes Jack groaned.

"He's waking up!" announced Jessica.

His whole family was standing around his bed, his mother hugging and kissing him.

"Don't you ever do that again!" she said indignantly, yet she looked happy and relieved as well.

"What happened?"

"I found you lying on the kitchen floor when I came in," replied

Kyle.

Jack could hardly remember what had caused him to wind up in the hospital, and the picture was slowly clearing up.

"The doctors don't know what made you pass out. Thank God you're completely healthy," said Jessica shrilly.

"Don't you remember *anything?*" asked Kyle.

Jack tried to focus. He could vaguely remember broken glass and… "Something was burning," he said slowly. Then it came back to him. He looked in fright at his chest and breathed in relief when he saw that his skin was still in one piece.

"Jack, what's wrong?" asked his father.

"Nothing," he said quickly. "I just thought I got…cut…by the broken glass. When can I come back home?" he asked, changing the subject.

"The doctors say you've got to stay here overnight for observation, and then you're good to go.

***

"The kid is starting to develop his powers."

"Can he control them yet?"

"No. He has no idea what's going on."

"Then what is the problem?"

"I think he's like his brother."

"Think?" Thomas's voice was full of frustration. "Why's that?"

"I'm almost sure I saw a blue flash when his powers went on autopilot."

"Pretty sure!?" yelled Thomas. "That's not good enough! I need you to be sure—"

"But I'm definitely sure I saw red," interrupted Brian calmly.

Thomas remained silent for a while. Finally he spoke in an unusually serene tone. "When do you think he is going to be alone again?"

"Tonight. He's staying at the hospital until tomorrow morning."

"Good. Then we go tonight."

***

Moonlight was streaming into the room through the second-story window of the hospital where Jack had been born. Silence was all that could be heard. Jack was fast asleep, unaware of the danger he was in.

Outside, in the empty parking lot under the building, a gust of black wind, darker than night, came hurling from the shadows of the trees through the cold, still air. It smoothly filtered into the quiet parking area. The flickering light of the fluorescent cylinders cast their harsh light upon the shapeless figure. It was touching the tarred ground but still seemed to be hovering. Slowly, it began to form the shape of a human body. The arms and legs were distorted, and there was no face, only two icy white eyes that shimmered vacantly. The fingers came into focus as though being projected through a lens being adjusted. Features began to etch themselves, giving the being a hollow face. Two dilated pupils faded into the blank eyes. Skin developed.

While the figure transformed into his natural human form, another obscure gust plunged into the parking lot. Seconds later, there was another, and another. Sounding like indistinct whispers, they altered into people.

There were seven of them, all wearing leather coats and gloves. The first to arrive spoke. "You take care of the guards." He gestured to one of the others, who nodded in acknowledgement and walked away swiftly, blending into the placid darkness. "You two get a car from somewhere. I want *you* to cut off the security system. Everything: CCTVs, alarms—make sure it's all out. Someone will definitely screw up and show themselves—we don't need that kind of nonsense. Max, you and Brian are coming with me." Thomas smirked. "We're going to visit the kid."

Jack woke suddenly to find someone standing over him. He sat up at once and tried to see the person's face, but it was too dark.

"We have to get out of here *right now!*" she said urgently. Jack didn't know who she was, but her voice sounded familiar.

"Who are—" he started.

Then she turned on the light and started shoving Jack's few belongings into a bag. "There are people after you, and they're going to be here any second now."

Jack was stunned.

"I know you." He pointed at her, flummoxed. "You're the one from those weird dreams I've been having. This is crazy—have we met before?"

"No."

"Then how do you explain…wait…what are you doing?" Jack was only now realizing that there was a stranger in his hospital room, packing his things in the middle of the night. "You said someone was after me—what would anybody want from me?"

"There's no time." The girl pulled Jack onto his feet and spoke anxiously. "If we don't get out of here *now*, they are going to get you, and God knows what they will do to you just to get their hands on that coin!"

"Wha—" Jack shook his head, perplexed.

"Xelticus."

"How do you know about that?" He stared at her.

"I heard that someone had it and then I…tracked you down."

"How!?"

"We have to leave!" she urged him impatiently. "I know this is really confusing—"

"Yeah." Jack nodded frantically.

"But if we—"

Footsteps sounded in the corridor. The two of them fell silent instantaneously and looked toward the closed door.

"Come on!" she whispered.

"You want to jump out the window?" said Jack when he saw her standing by the window.

"No!" she said indignantly. "Hold my hand."

Jack looked at her, confused, but did as she asked. "Okay… What now?"

The handle twisted slowly with a soft squeak. They stared at it, and Jack's heart started to thump heavily, creating a pit in his stomach. He did not know what to expect—none of this made any sense.

The door shifted open and Thomas walked in. "Where is he? Are you sure this is the right room?"

"Yeah, I'm positive," replied Brian. Max looked at him

disapprovingly.

Thomas eyed the covers lying on the floor. The room was empty.

"How the *hell* did he get out of here?" He kicked over the small cabinet that stood beside the bed. "How could he possibly know that—" He stopped in his ire and thought. "Vanessa," he said at once. Thomas sighed and turned his head slightly. "Looks like we've got to go with plan B." He looked out of the window dangerously. "Let's go home." A malicious smile spread across his face.

***

"What the hell just happened!?" asked Jack timidly. He was standing in his dark room, still holding hands with Vanessa.

"I teleported."

"What!? What do you…how did—"

"You didn't discover your abilities yet, did you?" She seemed rather amused.

"Abilities?" He raised his eyebrows and stared at her in amazement.

"You have supernatural abilities," she said simply.

Jack moved his mouth, but no words came out. He felt completely lost.

The girl giggled. "You'll understand everything in *due time.*"

"Yeah…when everything is supposed to make sense, right?" Jack recognized the ironic quote from the letter he had received from her with the silver key. "I can't wait."

"Where is the key I sent you?" She was a little calmer now but still seemed quite nervous.

"In the drawer behind you."

She slid open the drawer and pulled out the necklace with the key chiming on it gently. "This is keeping it safe?" She held it up. "A cat could find it here!"

"Well—"

"Wear it!" She threw it to him. "Where's the coin?"

"Guess," he said satirically as he secured the key around his neck.

Once again she delved in the drawer. "Catch."

"Why would anybody want this coin? What's so special about it?"

"It's complicated."

"What do we do now?"

She walked over to him and grabbed his hand. Everything swirled around them. Jack's head felt as though it were being compressed, and his eyes felt as though they were squinting, although the image remained focused. Colors blended into each other and, within moments, his room whirled into somewhere else. He was thrown forcefully onto a carpeted floor.

"Sorry, I'm a little rusty when I'm under pressure," the girl said.

"No problem." That was the least of his worries. Jack rose. "Where are we?" he asked, looking around at the old-fashioned chandeliers radiating golden light onto the upholstered chairs surrounding the small square dining table. The lounge opposite was furnished with a leather couch and a matching chair, a plasma screen, and a low Oregon pine coffee table.

"At my uncle's house," she responded.

"So I assume he knows about your…powers." It felt odd to say it out loud.

She smiled.

"Vanessa!" her uncle walked into the dining room, where they had just arrived. "How did it go?"

"Fine."

"Great." He smiled and turned to Jack. "You must be Jack." Vanessa's uncle put his hand forward. "I'm Ivan."

- CHAPTER FIVE -

XELTICUS

"Er…nice to meet you." Jack shook Ivan's hand.

"Come on, let's have a seat. I'm sure you've got a lot of questions." Ivan seemed like a kind person, but he looked rather nervous (though he obviously tried to hide it). "Would you like something to eat or drink?"

"Just some water, thanks."

Vanessa disappeared through the corridor into the kitchen.

"Ask away," said Ivan benignly, sitting on the chair in the lounge, leaving Jack to sit on the couch.

"All right, what about my parents? I mean, by tomorrow they will definitely find out that I'm not at the hospital. My mom's going to freak out and probably end up there herself."

Ivan chuckled. "Don't worry about it—everything will be taken care of."

Jack looked at him as though saying that he was not satisfied with this answer. He had just met the man, so his word meant nothing to Jack.

"I will have a word with your father," he explained. "Ben."

"You know my father?"

"Yep. We're old friends."

Jack was not quite sure what to believe anymore, but he did not say it. For now, all he wanted to do was listen and find out as much as possible about this utterly unexpected turn of events.

"You don't believe me, do you?" It was as though Ivan had read Jack's mind.

"No…sure I do," said Jack reassuringly.

"If you're always such a bad liar, that's really good."

Jack started to feel uncomfortable—even more than before.

"Your dad and I used to go to high school together. That's when all this weird stuff started happening. Ben was the first one of us to discover his abilities. We were neighbors at the time, and one day—early in the morning, about an hour before we took the bus to school—I heard his mother scream." Happiness appeared on his face at the recollection, and he half smiled. "So… I ran outside to see what was happening." He paused for a second. "Your grandmother was on the porch of their house, on her knees, crying hysterically. Ben was lying on the floor covered in flames. We thought he'd been burned alive. I didn't know what to do. I mean, I was so shocked and scared—he was my best friend. I thought he was dead. He just lay there motionless…burning."

Jack saw that Ivan truly believed this bizarre story. Nevertheless, after being teleported, Jack had an open mind about what he was hearing.

"I thought that there was some sort of terrible accident. And suddenly, he started moving. He just pushed himself up with his arms, slowly got up, and looked around. All you could see of his face was an outline and blood-red eyes staring around. So then the flames just faded out, and his clothes were wrecked—holes were singed everywhere, black marks on his face…and your dad just stood there, startled, without a scratch." Ivan paused again when Vanessa re-entered the lounge with a tray carrying three tall glasses and two short, fat jugs filled to the brim, one with ice water and one with freshly made lemonade. The thin fragments of pulp were still settling. "Thanks, Vanessa. You should try Vanessa's lemonade. It's better than any other."

Vanessa smiled proudly, while pouring herself a glass, and sat on the couch as well. Jack found it hard to believe that his father had some kind of powers. Why had he never heard of anything about this before? He had known his father his whole life of course, and someone else in his family obviously ought to have known something—or was this a secret that his father had kept from everyone except for the people who had found out on their own? And how could he know that Ivan was telling the truth about his father?

"I know it's all still sort of hard to believe, but bear with me until the end," Ivan said.

"I'm not going anywhere."

Ivan poured himself a glass of lemonade and filled Jack's with the beverage as well. "The sugar is good for the shock. Teleporting for the first time is quite…well, you know. Have some water afterward. Anyway…" He proceeded with the anecdote.

"Turns out that Dad can make fire out of nothing at all."

Jack looked at Vanessa, who responded with a look that said, "I told you so."

"So his parents wanted to keep the whole thing a secret because they didn't want any unnecessary attention. He asked me to do the same and, of course, I didn't say a word to anyone else. The only people who knew about this incident were my parents and me and your dad and his parents. By the time other people—who had heard something—came outside, it was only to find Ben and his mother hugging. They were told that Ben had caught fire because of an accident with the gas stove. They just said that they weren't sure what had happened and that it was a miracle that he had not gotten hurt.

"A few days later, I caught on fire too—same idea. To cut a long story short, within three months or so there were eight of us at school who had the exact same abilities. All of us had developed them when we were around eighteen years old. So we formed a group. And we kept it all a secret—and we all went to the same school because it was the only one in our area. That's how we all became friends.

"Now, one of the guys from the group decided to find out if anybody in his family had ever had powers. He wanted to know if this thing was hereditary. So he started doing research, and he dug as deep as he could to reach the roots of his family tree. All this is still back in high school—our last year. Ten years later, he calls up all the guys that used to be in the group for an urgent meeting at his house." Ivan swallowed half of his drink and set the glass on the well-kept table. Jack thought that the story must be really long if this was the cut version. He noticed Vanessa grinning, from the corner of his eye, as though sharing his thoughts.

"It turns out that his ancestors had the same gifts as us and that they had made a pact among themselves and a few others with abilities to protect some kind of "sacred" stone. And if that stone were to fall into the wrong hands, it would bring "darkness upon the land"—not that it would bring an apocalypse, but you get the idea. He managed to get all this information from a book which his great, great, great, whatever grandfather wrote. *Il Libro di Regali,* The Book of Gifts. Somehow he figured out the location of the stone, somewhere really hard to get to. And it also stated that only someone with the correct bloodline can open whatever the stone is kept in. We all agreed that the stone should stay where it was because it seemed like it had been a pretty good hiding place for centuries. Then we discovered that someone was after it, and even if whoever it was may not have had evil intentions, well—that amount of power can never be controlled. Hence we got the stone before the other person did, and we decided to carry on with the legacy.

"We forged eight identical coins out of pure silver, and I know this sounds crazy but we had to do it so that the coins were not like anything else. We each put a drop of our own blood into the mixture."

Jack found this greatly appalling and couldn't avoid the look of dismay that ensued.

"We did that so that the door that we built could only be opened with our coins. It's made of stone and is part of a cave wall which is now a tourist attraction. It can only be unlocked if all eight coins are used—it's impossible to do it otherwise. Behind that door, there is a box which was made from the silver that we had left after molding the coins. Only one key can open that box, which contains the stone."

In a way this all sounded familiar to Jack, protecting the coin so well.

"The guy who is looking for you, his name is Thomas. He

wants the stone and that's why he needs you, because of your coin."

Neither of them spoke for a while. Jack didn't have much to say. He just sat quietly and absorbed the overwhelming number of details. Ivan got up at once. "I almost forgot," he murmured and walked away, out of sight. Jack and Vanessa both waited for Ivan to return; they sat quietly like two fish in a bowl. Finally, after a short wait that felt relatively long, Ivan returned holding a large photo album under his arm.

"I told you I had proof that I was telling the truth. Here it is." He dropped the aged book on the wood surface with a heavy thump. The pages had yellowed with time, and Ivan turned to a page to show him the sepia photograph of himself and Ben at their graduation. "Your dad has the same picture; I figured he probably showed it to you before, so you may recognize it."

Jack did recognize it, but was still not fully satisfied. "Okay," he said slowly. "But what about the…fire…thing."

Ivan raised his hand in front of him and flicked it open. Orange-red flames burst out and danced ceremoniously around his fingers. He closed his hand into a fist, and the fire vanished. "Believe it all now?" asked Ivan, grinning.

"Uh huh." Jack was enthralled. "Oh, I still have another question," he said as he snapped back to reality.

"Ask."

"What does *Xelticus* mean?"

"The one who found out all about his ancestors and their brief history with the stone, his name was Michael Xelticus. He founded the idea of protecting the stone, so we named it after him.".

"And the star represents the eight members of the…club."

"It's as simple as that."

Jack turned to Vanessa, who had been listening silently until now, leaning her head and arm on the armrest, her right leg folded on the couch.

"How did you get into my dreams, and why am I the one who should be keeping the key?"

"About the dreams," she said, straightening up. "I guess I sort of…*teleported* into your mind somehow. I don't really understand that part myself. And about the key, they would never think that you have it. Hell, they still think it's with them. You are the best hiding place."

Jack awoke to find Ivan sitting alone in the kitchen, eating breakfast.

"Morning," he said when he saw Jack. "There's bread over there." He pointed to a dusty shelf. "The toaster is still hot if you want to use it."

"Thanks." Jack slipped four slices into the hot compartments. "Ivan, did you speak to my dad yet?" He feared what might happen if his mother arrived at the hospital to find an empty bed. One of the nurses would most likely tell her that he must have run away.

"Yes, I only got off the phone a few minutes ago. I took care of everything."

"Do you mind if I give him a call? I don't have my cell on me." Jack was still slightly suspicious about the situation, even though all the signs signaled otherwise. He still needed some form of hard proof.

"Sure, the phone's right over there."

Jack raised the receiver and dialed the number to his father's cell phone. There was no answer. During the second attempt, he remembered that his dad's phone had been sent in for repairs. He tried calling the landline, but there was no answer. He figured that everybody had already left for work.

"No answer?"

Jack shook his head.

"I almost forgot." Ivan snapped his fingers. "Ben left a message for you. Um…he said, 'Sit tight and take care.'"

Jack smiled in relief. His father, knowing him well enough to consider that he would be doubtful, had left a message to set his mind at rest. "Sit tight and take care" was what his dad had told him on his first day of school, when Jack had refused to stay alone in the unfamiliar classroom. "I'll be back before you know it," his dad had reassured him.

"You look relieved," said Ivan, noticing the change in Jack's face.

"So what's next?" asked Jack, avoiding the comment.

"You are going to start your training today or tomorrow. That depends on your teacher."

"What training?"

"Finish your breakfast."

***

Ivan opened the front door and stepped out. Jack followed. "Wow!" he exclaimed as he walked into the open air. The wooden abode was surrounded by robust mountains, and many were blanketed in trees. The scenic landscape was all that could be seen. On one side of the house stood a huge willow swathed with branches that reached the earth, creating a thick curtain of emerald leaves.

Opposite was a valley, the clear water flowing peacefully into the teeming shade of the forest. The sky was clear, and the only thing hovering overhead was the vivid sun, aside from the cheeping birds that soared above their heads intermittently and could still be heard when unseen. The sight was dazzling.

"It's something isn't it?" Ivan said proudly.

"This is amazing."

"I'm guessing you are going to enjoy the waterfall. Maybe Vanessa will take you there later on."

Jack was still gazing into the distance. "This is all yours?"

"I bought it a few years ago. We should get going." Ivan started walking down the small hill that the house stood on. Jack was rather surprised. Ivan did not give the impression of someone who was arrogantly swimming in a pool of gold coins like Uncle Scrooge in *Duck Tales*.

It took them twenty minutes of driving on a wide dirt road to get to the highway. "Where are we going?" asked Jack.

"I want you to meet someone," replied Ivan. For a while after that, neither of them spoke. Jack watched the cars swoosh by, the sound strongly resembling the mysterious noise he had heard on the night of his birthday for the first time. Life had taken an outright unforeseen twist. "What training were you talking about before?"

"You'll see," said Ivan inscrutably, staring at the road ahead. "Music?"

"Sure." Naturally, Jack was unsatisfied with this answer, and his curiosity was exceedingly thirsty. Finally, Ivan turned onto a side road and, within a short while, stopped in front of a restaurant in an old-fashioned town. "Come on."

Both of them had just eaten breakfast, so Jack figured that this was where he was going to meet the mysterious person. "Take a seat," Ivan told Jack, doing so himself. The table was by the window, and Jack watched the pedestrians walking on the pavement, most of them greeting each other as they passed by.

"Would you like a menu?" asked a waitress, politely holding out a couple of laminated papers.

"No thank you, we just came to say hi to Eric. Do you mind calling him for us?"

"Sure, no problem." She went to the kitchen, and then another waiter came to their table.

"Ivan?" he exclaimed, looking at him in disbelief. "What are you doing here!?" He was about the same age as Jack and had short dark hair. Ivan stood up and hugged him, patting him hard on the back.

"Long time no see, huh?"

"Yeah, I'd like to introduce you to someone. Eric, this is Jack—Jack, Eric."

"Hey, man, good to meet you." They shook hands.

"Likewise."

Eric turned back to Ivan. "So what brings you here?"

"About that—I want you to train Jack," said Ivan frankly.

"*What!?*" demanded Eric and Jack in concert.

"I'm not training anybody, man. I don't do that."

"But you're good at it."

"But I hate it," retorted Eric impertinently.

"Thomas has six of the coins. I have one and he has one."

"Take his coin and keep it safe with yours," said Eric as if solving the problem.

Ivan looked at him in disagreement.

"Is he a New Blood?" asked Eric at last, caving in.

"Yes."

"What does he do?"

"Same as me."

"At least it will be easier than it was with Vanessa."

Ivan nodded in agreement, and Jack just sat there and listened while they spoke about him as if he were not present.

"Jack, right?" Eric turned back to face him, though not nearly as enthused as earlier.

"Yeah," he responded, finally joining the conversation.

"Tomorrow morning at six o'clock, we start training," he said curtly.

"Absolutely—why not?" murmured Jack.

"Thank you so much, Eric. This is a great deal of help."

"Just don't turn this into a habit, all right?"

"Last one for now, I promise," said Ivan humorously.

"That's funny, Ivan. Can you ask Vanessa to drop him off at the hangar?"

"Yeah, will do."

"Do you guys want to order anything? It's on the house."

"No thanks," said Jack.

"We just had breakfast," Ivan added.

"All righty, then, I've got to get back to work."

"Thanks, Eric," Ivan called after him.

"Yeah, yeah…whatever," he mumbled, brandishing his hand over his shoulder.

"What just happened?" inquired Jack when Eric was out of sight.

"You are going to learn how to use your powers."

"Powers?"

"How did you get to the hospital?" Ivan asked.

"So that's how it starts, huh?"

"With some people. You're just like your old man. But with training, you will be able to master your abilities a lot faster. Plus, you won't burn any furniture or other things while getting the hang of it."

***

"So what exactly do I do after I learn to use my abilities?" Jack asked once they were already halfway up the dirt road that led to the magnificent plot. "Why do I need to get the knack of things quicker than usual?"

"We are going to have to stop this whole thing once and for all."

"How long has this been going on?"

Ivan sighed. "Since 1981…."

"Then what changed? Why now?"

He looked at the road ahead and sighed yet again, although more grim this time. Something about the question seemed to trouble him. He appeared to be somewhat hurt, but tried to hide it.

Jack wanted to ask what was the matter, but felt that it was none of his business.

"Well…" Ivan hesitated, trying to find the words. "We didn't stop Thomas until now because he has never *actually* been able to get the stone. Now that he has six coins and knows almost exactly where the other two are, it's only a matter of time until he gets his hands on them." He parked the car, and they stepped out into the strong breeze that carried dead leaves on its back effortlessly. Jack thought about it for a moment.

"Ivan?"

"Yes?" he said distractedly, his thoughts elsewhere.

"Do you mind if I look at the place?" He had decided to change the subject, realizing that he had stepped on a sensitive point but unable to put his finger on it.

"Knock yourself out, Dora." Ivan vanished into the house.

Jack looked around and tried to decide which way to go; then he walked toward the valley. Until the sun set, he stayed by the river, exploring the area near it. Captivated, he watched the spherical ball of fire reflecting brilliantly in the crimson water, sparkling with millions of glinting diamonds that turned into stars as the sky faded to black. The sun drifted away to reveal a glimmering moon, and water flowing serenely, glowing a deep sapphire. Vanessa suddenly appeared out of thin air behind Jack.

"What are you doing here?"

"Just sitting." He was staring at the water as it slid out of sight.

"My uncle told me you'd been here since this morning,"

"Pretty much… Where have *you* been the whole day?" asked Jack, still staring at the silent stream.

"All over the world."

The two laughed lightly. "Do you want to see something cool?" she asked.

"Always."

"Get up."

Jack looked back at her. "Okay." As soon as he got to his feet, Vanessa put her hand on his shoulder, and he felt as though he were being sucked into an enormous vacuum. And then the world around him disappeared. The loud sound of liquid splashing incessantly drowned the hum of the wind and the chirring of the crickets. They were standing on an uneven surface of sturdy stone behind a translucent screen of water.

"Are we behind the waterfall?" asked Jack, impressed.

"What do you think?"

"You were right. It is cool."

"I come here when I want to be alone. You know, 'cause nobody else can get here that easily."

"How does it feel being able to be anywhere you want?"

"You just feel…free." There was excitement in her voice. "I hear you're starting training tomorrow, learning how to use your powers."

"Yeah, is it hard?"

"Not that bad—you know how Eric is a little—"

"No, I mean using powers… Is it difficult?"

"At first it is. But then you get used to it. It's kind of like learning to walk. Get up, fall down…"

"So I guess I just pass out a few times and…take it from there. One step at a time. I'm doing pretty well so far."

***

Jack felt the grass beneath his feet transform into a solid brick floor. It was still quite dark on this early morning, when he and Vanessa teleported. Aside from the distant echoes of whistling engines, the airport was hushed and the gray sky steadily grew brighter from the horizon.

"Good morning!" said Eric in a loud, enthusiastic voice. "I'm glad you could make it on time." He glanced at his watch and then looked up at Vanessa. "You can pick him up in about three hours."

"All right—good luck," she told Jack and then, without further ado, dissolved into the mellow breeze.

"C'mon." Eric led the way to a white plane hangar, the weak light of the early sunrise reflecting off it brightly. "This is the best place you could practice how to use your powers. No one ever comes to this part of the airport. At least we're going to put it to good use." He came to a halt in front of the locked entrance and raised his hand above the padlock clinging to the chains that tightly sealed the two large doors. A soft *clunk* sounded, and the lock sprang open. Eric raised his other hand and began to move both his arms sideways. At first, it seemed as though he were trying to part the air, but then the doors began to slide open.

Jack watched in amazement as the doors shifted aside. There was just no end to it—the surprises kept coming out of nowhere. Only a little less than three months ago, he had been sitting in Mr. Brown's dull classroom, and now he was spending his time with people who could move objects without touching them, travel across the world in seconds, and generate fire from nothing. Everything was changing so fast, it was like waking up one morning and stepping through a portal into a whole new universe.

He followed Eric into the vast empty space that would house two Seven-Four-Sevens. They entered and the doors shut behind them. Jack looked back and watched the faint light drain away.

Eric thrust his hand toward a heavy switch, and the hangar filled with an ashen glow.

"All right, let's see what you got." He turned to face Jack.

"I can't do…er…anything with my powers." He felt slightly embarrassed. "Yet," he added quickly.

"Nothing?" Eric asked. Disappointment was clearly evident in his tone.

"At all," replied Jack, raising his eyebrows.

"Okay…" Eric said slowly. "Just try—focus."

Jack raised his hand and stared at it. He balled it into a firm fist and then, after a few seconds, he spread it wide open, hoping for the flames to burst out just as they had for Ivan.

Nothing happened.

There was still silence.

Eric had been gazing at Jack hopefully, but then…

"This is useless," he said abruptly. "Let me think. Um…" He bit his lip in intense thought. "I got it!" His face lit up with an idea, and Jack could imagine a light bulb blinking above his head.

Suddenly, Eric threw his arm forward. Within split seconds, a transparent, circular pulse emitted from his palm and swooped through the air, growing rapidly as it neared Jack. Once it hit him, it melted into the atmosphere and sent him hurtling backward, slamming him into the steel wall behind him so hard that he bounced off it before falling hard to his knees.

"What the hell was that!?" Jack struggled, leaning on the floor with one hand, the other at his chest. He found it quite hard to breathe after the tough, painful hit. Eric ignored the question.

"Come on," he barked impatiently. "Get up!"

"What? Are you—"

But before Jack could finish his sentence, Eric raised two fingers. Jack's feet were just above the floor. Eric waved his arm and sent him flying across the hangar and crashing into the opposite wall, this time sideways. Jack dropped to the floor, preventing the fall from being worse by breaking it with his hands. *Why is he doing this?* Jack thought as he slowly heaved himself onto his feet. Suddenly, he was pushed flat to the cold ground and found himself sliding along it, his arms shielding his face to make the next collision with a barrier as painless as possible.

"Wait!" Jack breathed heavily, but Eric did the same thing again. "STOP IT!" he bellowed indignantly. He was ignored and lifted into midair, with just a look, and then left to drop with a harsh thud.

Jack began to feel hot. He was so incensed that he was being bounced off the walls like a bouncing ball for no apparent reason. And then another powerful wave of energy glided toward him. Instinctively, while lying on the floor, he lifted his arm to shield himself. A surge of immense heat flowed through his entire body and, to his amazement, spouted and mushroomed into an orb. The coiling flames clashed with Eric's lucent pulse. The impact emitted by the two forces combined and, with a fantastic ripple, faded into nothing.

It felt to Jack that the whole thing had moved in slow motion. He stood up, and Eric started clapping, the reverberation ringing loudly. "And there's lesson number one," he said ecstatically.

***

Richard was hurrying down Lance Avenue and turned sharply onto River Lane. Allison was racing two steps behind. "Which house do they live in?" she panted breathlessly.

"It's that big white one." Richard pointed to the Sullivans' home as he and Allison neared it. They came to a sudden halt in front of the brick path. A tile from one of the stone stairs was broken and lay unevenly on the step below. Half of the wooden banister that ran across the side was almost falling onto the black blotch burned onto the grass, desperately clinging to the last strands of wood that attached it to its other half.

Richard quickly ran up the stairs and opened the front door. Aghast, he slowly moved onto the bed of splinters and shards of glass that hid the face of the tiled floor. A seemingly deafening *crunch* echoed with every step they took. The pictures that were meant to occupy the white walls lay smashed on the floor; others were hanging from their frames, swinging from side to side. "Oh my God!" gasped Allison, horror struck, as she entered.

"Thomas was already here," Richard mumbled, peering into the kitchen to see the table lying on its side and a cupboard door falling off its hinges to reveal a set of broken cups. "And not so long ago, by the looks of it." He placed his foot on a shattered porcelain vase that was still lying on the floor.

"We should go to Ivan," suggested Allison anxiously, gazing wide eyed at the horrid sight.

"You're right." Richard turned to face her, tearing his eyes from the scene. "We should hurry." The two of them swiftly paced into the open air and began their journey.

- CHAPTER SIX -

INIQUITY

A fist knocked monotonously on the Dawsons' front door.

"Who is it?" growled Mr. Dawson, awakening from his sleep yet still keeping his eyelids shut.

No one answered.

Again, three soft *thuds* sounded through the wooden slab.

"Who's there?" asked Mr. Dawson indignantly, turning his head to face the door, staring, as if waiting for it to reply.

Still, silence.

Once again, the fist hit the door, this time a little harder.

"Damn it," he murmured as he lifted himself off the couch. "Probably some deaf guy," he said to himself while dragging his brown slippers along the wooly carpet. "I hope not. Then I'd feel bad about what I said." A slight twinge of guilt grew at the thought but immediately disappeared when the person outside pounded on the door yet again.

"I'm coming! I'm coming!" whined Mr. Dawson loudly. Sliding the bolt out of the socket with a metallic chime he flung the door open. Facing him was a rather pale man, dressed in black, with a long leather coat hanging from his broad shoulders.

"George Dawson?"

Mr. Dawson did not answer. Instead, he asked uncouthly, "Who are you?"

"Oh, I'm so sorry," said the man, shaking his head faintly. "How rude of me." Stretching out his hand he gave an unsettling smiled. "My name is Thomas."

***

Jack had already been training to use his abilities for the past three weeks, and today was his last lesson. In a way it reminded him of his final exams (although this was a lot more fun). The last time he had spoken to his parents was two nights before; Kyle and Jessica were out but sent their regards. His father had phoned Ivan, but since then he hadn't been able to get a hold of them, even on their cell phones. Also Ivan's attempt had failed. He had been wondering whether Kyle and Jessica knew where he was and what he was doing. Had his mother and father told them he had strange abilities, or had they decided to keep it all a secret and fabricate a reason why he was away from home for so long? He missed Claire and thought about calling her, but he did not want to lie to her about where he was. And the truth would simply cause him to sound like a crazy person.

He was about to exit the house and wait outside for Vanessa to come get him. Before he reached the front door, the air before his eyes quivered as though heat was emanating from the parquet floor. Just then Vanessa stepped, from nowhere, before Jack. It was something he was already used to by now.

"Are you ready?" she asked, enthusiastically beaming at him.

"Yeah. Why are you dressed like that?" he added, noticing that she was wearing a thick pink fur coat, a pair of woolen gloves, and a gray beanie. Her shoulders were level with her ears, and she was shivering slightly and red nosed.

"You'll see—by the way, you might want this." She handed him a fleece jacket. "You won't be able to move if you wear what I am wearing."

"Okay. And what is that for?" he asked suspiciously, pointing to the video camera clutched in her hand.

"What, you thought I would miss this?" She looked at him as though it was an odd question. "Give me your hand."

Jack gripped her extended hand and grinned at how awkward she looked in that fat jacket, almost like a snowman. She gave him an annoyed look and, with a sudden jolt, their surroundings transformed from a sitting room into snow. Jack was standing beside Vanessa in what felt like an extremely spacious freezer. Icy mist surrounded them, and anything farther than fifty feet could not be seen.

The place was entirely vacant aside from them and one other person, to whom Vanessa was already striding through the heavy blanket of snow that rose above their ankles.

"Jack!" Eric called out to him through the billowing wind, snowflakes filling the atmosphere like bleached soot. Jack moved forward, leaving two furrow-like trails behind him. "All right," bellowed Eric. Above the roaring wind Jack could barely hear him. "Today is your final lesson in training, so what we're going to do…" Eric stopped talking and raised both arms momentarily. Right away, the howling and rushing of the wind that had filled their ears only a few seconds ago was gone. The icy flakes, which had been swirling rapidly, prickling their faces like cold needles, had calmed and begun to settle. Jack understood that Eric had created some sort of invisible force field. He had an interesting image of the three of them inside a small snow globe that someone had just stopped shaking.

"As I was saying…" Eric continued, now that nature was not interrupting him. "What we're going to do is *fight*."

"You mean…you and me?" Jack was surprised, yet the idea did sound like something Eric would think of, now that Jack had gotten to know him a little more.

Eric simply nodded.

"No, I'm not fighting you," Jack said sternly.

"Why?" asked Eric, as impatiently as usual.

"Because…"

Jack tried to think of the words to explain himself while being stared at with uncertainty. The reason was obvious, and he finally mustered the words to say, "I could hurt you. We don't have the same ability and, in case you haven't noticed yet, I burn stuff. You're the one who taught me to do that over the past few weeks."

"Don't worry about me. I won't get hurt," Eric reassured him confidently.

"But—" Jack started.

"Take a shot at me."

"Wha— no!"

"Dude, don't you remember the first lesson that we had? You hit me with the best you had, and I blocked it."

"Oh, yeah…I forgot about that. It feels like such a long time ago."

"All right, let's do this thing."

"If you insist…" He stepped back and lifted both hands. Jack felt an immense surge of heat surge through his arms as he shot a perfect globe of fire from his palms.

Eric just stood there as the blazing orb flew at him, and not at a particularly high speed.

'You're going to have to do better than that," Eric dodged the blow. "Surprise me. This is combat, not training. And you're going to have to beat me in this cold, with your heat."

"All right."

"Don't just stand there like a block of ice, hit me Jack" goaded Eric. "If you can."

Again, Jack tried his luck. But in this cold his fingers were already numb, he couldn't feel his cheeks ears or nose, and he was not nearly dressed well enough for this weather. Clearly this final exercise was meant to push him to the limits.

Taking a lazy step sideways, Eric moved aside from the feeble fireball and shook his head with a sly smirk. "Here, I'll show you—"

The snow rippled around Jack like a tornado and sent him hurting up in the air in circles. When he landed on his back, he felt queasy and felt a headache coming on. However, thanks to the numbing cold, even that he could barely feel.

"Let's reminisce, just like our first lesson," taunted Eric.

And Jack knew exactly what he meant, so before Eric's next wild attack could collide with Jack and send him flying all over the place like their first lesson, Jack blocked and threw himself sideways for another hit he knew was coming. It missed him closely. Jack sent a stream of heat toward Eric, knowing it wouldn't throw him off his game, but it did give Jack a second to get to his fist and attack again.

Turned out that a duel could be quite fun. Soon the "arena" had become a rush of heat and snow and invisible forces. While Vanessa kept teleporting this way and that to avoid being hit by a deflected attack or a splash of freezing water from all the snow that was beginning to melt around them. She too was enjoying herself, watching the other two with a smile, cheering for this one, and then for that.

And then everything that happened seemed to be in a slow blur. Vanessa backed away, shutting her eyes and turning her head. Eric was knocked square in the chest, the snow around him exploded like a blitzkrieg, and Jack gaped in shock, still unable to believe what he had done. But when the small cloud of snow settled, Eric was standing in the same place, smiling with satisfaction. Jack let out a sigh of relief.

"Thought you got me, huh?" he asked happily, walking toward him.

"Hey, Vanessa."

Vanessa was recording the entire scene and giggling behind the camera, obviously at Jack's frightened reaction.

"So that's what you got the camera for—can't miss these treasured moments?" he asked sarcastically, now talking more to the lens than the person operating it.

She shrugged and continued to record, still smiling faintly.

"Ready to for round two?" asked Eric zealously, not hiding his excitement about what was about to happen. He most certainly enjoyed this duel, especially after having to teach Jack all this time. Jack knew that Eric considered this a splendid reward for all his hard work.

Eric shook his hands and cracked his neck from side to side, "This is going to be fun."

And without warning, the snow at Jack's feet trembled and exploded with a shrill *hiss*. He landed flat on his back with a hollow *thud*, his sight obscured by millions of bright snowflakes zooming silently. He tried to listen for Eric's usual witless laugh when he succeeded in such an act, yet the air was still, aside from the frosty dust. He listened hard for any other sound that might give away Eric's position, but there was none.

And then, through the pearl-white haze, he saw a tall shadow creeping nearer. Still lying on the wet ground, Jack aimed and, once again, felt the warm pulse of energy rush through him. But this time something unexpected happened, something that had never happened before. His entire body filled with a warmth unlike any other, and he felt stronger and more confident than ever before in his life. Striking blue flames lashed out, spinning gently yet powerfully. An unnatural glow beamed in every direction, dissolving the snow nearby with incredible ease. The lethal flames glided smoothly and dissolved like the snow around them and, when their destination was reached, plunged into it fiercely.

"ERIC!" Jack jumped to his feet and sprinted to Eric, who was lying face down in the cold deep snow that buried the ground beneath. Jack dropped to his knees beside him. "What have I done?" He was awestruck. He didn't know what to do; he had never meant to hurt his friend. During practice, Eric always told him that he must not be afraid to use his power to the fullest. Eric constantly kept an invisible shield around him to shelter him from the heat.

But now Jack knew that something was wrong. Eric's clothes were singed, and thin smoke was ascending quietly and slowly. Vanessa was still holding the camera in both hands, recording. She was bewildered and rooted to the spot.

"Come help me!" Jack shouted to her.

She blinked as if waking from a state of hypnosis and hurried to the spot where Eric lay motionless.

"Get us out of here! We have to take him to a hospital!"

"O—Okay." She was extremely shaky, and Jack knew that it was not because of the cold. Hands shivering, she gripped Eric's shoulder tightly.

"Hold my hand!" she urged Jack, and he did so immediately. "Wait…"

"What's wrong?"

Vanessa was looking around curiously.

"What are we waiting for? Come on, get us out of here!" bawled Jack indignantly. Panic started to sink in, and he blocked out any thought of the worst, keeping his mind blank. It made no sense to him that she was suddenly so calm about the matter and was looking around as if searching for a good picnic spot.

"He's fine," she said with relief, looking at Eric.

"FINE? Look at him! He's…" The words Jack needed did not exist. So instead of finishing the sentence, he just groaned irritably. He was amazed that Vanessa could say everything was *fine* when something was clearly wrong. He was simply baffled at this bizarre situation.

"The wind isn't blowing on us," she explained.

"So?" Jack was unable to see her point in his current state of mind.

"So, that means that his force field is still active, and it wouldn't be if he was…not fine."

"Are you sure? 'Cause he looks pretty—"

"I'm positive, Jack."

Eric moaned and rolled over slowly to reveal a face covered in what looked like an old man's badly shaven beard. He sat up and looked at Vanessa, then turned his eyes to Jack.

"What the hell was that?"

"I didn't mean to—I'm sorry," Jack stuttered apologetically.

Eric laughed weakly.

"Well done, mate." He gripped Jack's hand. "You won. You passed the test!"

Jack half smiled; he was still a little off-beat. He looked at Vanessa, who smiled and then stood.

"Now pull me up before my butt freezes," Eric told Jack in his usual dominant tone. The three of them dispersed into the wind, which began to howl again the moment they left.

***

"So what happens next?" Jack asked Ivan, once they were all seated at the dinner table after a hot shower. Outside, the sun was sinking into a pool of claret light, gushing through the clear windows, veiling the inside of the house with an auburn gleam.

"Ah," Ivan put down his fork and beamed at Jack. "I was waiting for that to come up." He sat up in his chair. "Now that you've finished your training, we are going to have to find a way to stop Thomas from getting his hands on that stone. And to do that, we need some sort of plan. Seeing as there isn't that much time left before he figures out where to get the last two coins, we have to start tonight, right after supper."

"By the way…" Jack wanted to ask something that had been on his mind. "Did you manage to get a hold of my parents?"

"Sorry Jack, nobody answers their phones. It just goes directly to voicemail. I also tried those numbers you left me for your brother's and sister's cell phones, and the call doesn't go through."

It wasn't like his parents and Jessica to be unavailable at all. Kyle, on the other hand, would turn off his cell and ignore the home phone if he was busy with anything important and didn't feel like answering talking to anybody on the phone—which is how Kyle always felt.

"Did you try calling them at work?" Jack glanced at his watch and stood up. "My dad should still be there." He paced to the phone and started dialing, straining his brain trying to remember the correct digits. Finally, it came to him, and he waited for someone to pick up on the other end of the line.

"Hello?" The woman who answered sounded surprised to get a call at this hour.

"Hi, I'm looking for Mr. Sullivan. It's his son Jack."

"Oh, um…he isn't here, but I haven't seen him at work for the past two days. I assumed he wasn't feeling well."

His father had been perfectly healthy the last time that he had spoken to him. "Thank you." Slowly Jack lowered the receiver.

"What is it?" asked Ivan, concerned.

"Er…he hasn't been at work the last two days." Jack was worried about his family now more than ever. "But they're okay, right?" he asked. Hoping to get the answer he desired, he looked at each one of the faces at the table. All looked uncomfortable, and a shrill silence lingered in the air. Only the clock in the kitchen continued to tick monotonously, the sound traveling stridently through the still air. "I mean, they have to be—don't they?" said Jack apprehensively, still looking from Ivan to Vanessa to Eric and back.

"Honestly, Jack…we don't know," said Ivan with unease.

"Vanessa, you can take me there just to check that—"

"No, it's too dangerous," said Ivan at once. "They could be waiting for you over there."

"But what if…something happened to them? What if Thomas—" He fell silent. The thought alone was terrible enough, and he avoided it with all his might. He didn't want to think about it, let alone say it out loud.

"No," said Ivan definitely. "He would never do anything like that."

"How can you be so sure?" asked Jack apprehensively.

"Because I can. I know him; he would never be able to do anything like that," said Ivan confidently, looking at his plate rather than at Jack.

Then Vanessa spoke for the first time. "He's right Jack, D—" she flinched. "Thomas would never do that." She looked away uncomfortably, avoiding looking in Jack's eyes.

Ivan looked at her for a moment and resumed staring at his half-empty plate. Again, it shimmered in his eyes, and his niece seemed to recognize it. It was the same sadness that Jack had seen when he'd asked about Thomas on their way back from meeting Eric, who sat so quietly that Jack had never seen him like this before.

"I can't just sit here and wait."

"We'll go tomorrow. It's safer in daylight, when there are lots of people around," said Ivan considerately.

"Then we have to go at about seven-thirty in the morning, when everybody leaves for work. Otherwise the neighborhood is dead until it's evening again," explained Jack, feeling slightly relieved, though the heavy weight on his chest filled him with angst.

"All right," agreed Ivan, the tension beginning to slacken.

"So we should be working on the plan until then, shouldn't we?" suggested Eric timidly.

Ivan got up. "Follow me." He led the way. The other three followed. They all seemed to have forgotten about the meal—it just wasn't that important anymore.

Ivan led them into a small room, on the other end of the quiet house, which was quite empty. A bright lamp was mounted on the ceiling, not matching the chandeliers that were suspended above in the rest of the house. In the center of the room stood a table with two chairs. Only blank papers and pencils lay on the table. The two shelves housed three large, badly rolled spreadsheets that looked like blueprints, and in the corner was a slim laptop resting on a small crooked three-legged table.

"All right," Ivan announced audibly when they had all entered. "We have got to work fast, so any ideas you guys have would be greatly appreciated." He shut the door.

Jack didn't know how much time had passed since they had begun discussing the various options for protecting the stone. There was no way of reaching it before Thomas did. They only had two coins, and attaining the other six was hopeless. Time appeared to be standing still, especially because there were no clocks in this hollow room. Jack and Eric were leaning against two adjoining walls, and Ivan was sitting on one of the wooden chairs, which creaked loudly each time he moved. It was painted in what resembled a dry layer of blue-green toothpaste, most of which had peeled off over the years. Vanessa balanced on the two hind "matchsticks" of her chair, which proved to be much stronger than they looked. She kept hold of the old wooden table to prevent herself from toppling over.

"Jack, are you all right? You haven't said a word since we got in here," Ivan asked unexpectedly.

"Yeah, I'm fine," he replied and resumed gawking at the scratched wooden floor. He usually thought up useful ideas for various types of things. But this was different. The current situation was nothing like a school assignment or the tasks around the house that his mother would often impose upon him and the rest of the family. His brain was numb; it was like walking out of a triple math lesson (which he was pleased he would never have to endure again). Only one thought occupied his blurred mind: the people he cared about most. *Is Mom okay? And Dad? What about Kyle and Jessy?*

The voice in his head was the only one he could hear as he watched the others' lips moving with no sound coming out. And then Claire's face slid into his mind.

"I've got to go use the phone," he informed the others and strolled hurriedly out the door.

Ivan hesitated then followed him. "Trying to get hold of your parents again?"

Jack was already punching in the number on the keypad. "I'm not calling my parents." "Then who—" Ivan was puzzled and didn't try to guess. He stood there and waited to see what would happen.

The call went directly to voicemail. Jack pushed down the button with his thumb instead of placing the receiver in the cradle—that would take too long, and time was becoming more and more valuable with every second that slipped away. He dialed Claire's cell number and felt the weight on his chest, which had been getting heavier, lift slightly as the receiver began to purr tediously.

"Hello?"

"Claire!" Jack sighed in relief. "I didn't manage to get through to your house—I'm so glad you're okay."

"Jack, are you all right?"

He could see her expression in his mind's eye as she spoke. "Er…" He didn't know how to answer that question. "Yeah, I guess." Hearing her voice lifted the rock that lay on his chest. However, it was plunged back into his heart with a heavy blow. "Listen, I don't know how to say this but—"

"That's weird." She was distracted by something.

"What? What is it?"

"I just got home, and all the lights are off and the door is locked."

"Claire, listen to me—CLAIRE!" he yelled into the receiver. Claire's short, frantic scream came from a distance, and the cell phone fell on the grass with a *thump*, a *crunch,* and static.

Jack dropped the receiver, and it dangled inches from the floor, being held aloft by its winding cord.

"What the hell just happened?" Ivan was gawping at him.

Jack looked into the man's serious face, anger burning within him. "They have Claire and her parents, my family." He spoke in a dangerously calm voice, clenching his jaw. "We have to go, right now—plan or no plan, I don't care."

Ivan nodded. "Fair enough. I'll call Vanessa and Eric."

Jack was more awake and alert than ever.

Now it was personal.

"Who's Claire?" Eric mumbled to Vanessa as they passed through the hall.

"His girlfriend," she whispered back.

"Oh…"

The four of them were just about to teleport out of the orderly dining room when a loud *crash* boomed from outside and someone called, "IVAN!"

"Richard?" Ivan sped out. The other three exchanged looks and hurried after. A man taller than Ivan was standing in the living room dripping water from his sopping clothes. His short black hair stuck to his forehead, mud was strewn on his face, and he was breathing heavily. "We all have to get out of here right now," he urged, stepping forward. From behind him a woman, looking just as bedraggled, appeared. She slowly paced forward and stood by Richard. With every step she took, a watery *squish* sounded from her drenched shoes.

"Allison?" Ivan looked at the woman.

"Hi." She was shivering, her blonde hair draped in front of her face, almost completely hiding her strong features.

"What's going on?" he asked the disheveled couple anxiously.

Richard looked anxiously over his shoulder. Jack heard it too, an unnatural rush of wind.

"Get inside." Richard slammed the door behind them. "They're coming—NOW. And Thomas is really pissed!"

"Right now?" Jack suddenly joined the conversation. He didn't know these people, and he most certainly did not care about introducing himself. All that mattered now was that Thomas had taken his family and Claire.

"Yes." Richard looked back at Ivan. "But the second-damn-worse thing is Max."

"That is worse. Max is a real pain in the—"

Smash.

A shapeless, raven-black figure with gleaming white eyes flooded violently through the window, sending shards of glass soaring in every direction.

Everyone in the room covered their faces instinctively. A jagged sliver cut Jack across his forearm.

"VANESSA!" Richard yelled as more dark figures blew in through every opening in the house, making new openings where possible, closing in.

"HOLD ON!" Vanessa shouted, and Jack grabbed hold of her ankle just in time to see the light drown and chaos swirl into a cold and blustery night. The stars were concealed by profuse gray clouds that sheathed the entire sky. Only now did he realize that it was pouring outside.

- CHAPTER SEVEN -

WHAT THEY DIDN'T KNOW

They all regrouped after being hurled ferociously into their new surroundings.

"Where are we?" Jack asked Vanessa.

"Part A of the plan," she replied loudly, to be heard above the wailing wind and splashing rain.

A bolt of lightning tore the sky and burned the image onto Jack's eyes. He looked ahead of him and saw a plain building that stood tall and wide. It was on the outskirts and looked like it had no life in it. Mostly since all the windows were tinted so that not even a silhouette could be seen inside. At the side of the building, on one of the top floors, was a large hole that tunneled right through.

"We have a plan," said Ivan, talking to Richard and Allison. "What we're going to do is—"

"Why don't you, er…hold that thought until the others get here?" interrupted Richard.

"Others?"

"They're on their way; they'll be here any minute now."

"We're already here," a deep voice boomed out of the shadows, but there was no one to be seen. Jack was expecting someone to appear from thin air—he had gotten used to the idea over the past few weeks. Instead, four figures emerged from behind the corner of the rectangular building, their feet splashing in the miniature river that filled the empty streets. The tallest figure was the one to whom the voice belonged. He was a large, muscular black man. It looked as though it would take a good swing with a sledgehammer to get him to budge. The moon's reflection could almost be seen on his bald head.

"Hi, I'm Tren." He held out his hand to Jack, who shook it firmly.

"Jack."

Tren did not loosen his grip and remained smiling. "Jack Who?" he asked in his menacing bass voice, turning his head a little to the side like a pigeon trying to get a better look.

"Sullivan." Jack felt somewhat unnerved.

Tren's smile faded, and a surprised expression of curiosity spread upon his face. He examined Jack, still not letting his hand loose from this unusually long handshake.

"Ben's kid!?" he said, mesmerized.

"Yep."

"Unbelievable." He straightened up. "You look just like your mother. By the way, how's Kyle and Jessy doing?"

Apparently, this man knew Jack's family from a long time ago.

"I don't know. Thomas took them; also my girlfriend and her parents." He felt the rage and hate toward Thomas smolder within.

"Took—what!?" Tren finally let go of Jack's hand and looked at Richard. "You didn't tell me nothing about the Sullivan family being kidnapped!"

"There was no time," Richard rejoined defensively. "We had to go warn Ivan. Besides, I only had one quarter on me."

Tren's wife took charge of the matter. "That's enough, you guys. Let's get moving—we got a lot to do and this ain't helping anybody." Her hair was still rather bushy in the showering rain. Jack could only imagine what it looked like when it was dry.

"Yeah, you right baby—this is my wife, Marisa. And my son, Mark"

"Nice to meet you," said Jack fretfully. Time was not waiting, and he was not focusing on anything else besides what they had come here to do.

"'Sup man?" Mark was like a smaller version of his father, with trimmed hair and an earring in his left ear. The only difference was that he was younger and did not look like a heavyweight wrestler (although he did seem to be following in his father's footsteps).

"Hey." Jack shook his hand firmly and briefly.

"Now, Tren?" said Ivan impatiently.

"Yeah, yeah, no time—sorry," he said quickly. "Last one. This is Ryan."

Ryan merely nodded. Slick black hair with a shade of dark blue almost completely covered one of his eyes which were shaded very lightly with black eyeliner and his skin was quite pale. Jack noted the black nail polish and skull ring.

"He only looks that young 'cause he joined us when he was what? Two?" He laughed. "Ivan, what's the plan?"

"Now that you guys are here, it will be a lot easier to get inside." He spoke while moving forward, all eyes fixed upon him. "Mark can open the door for us. Meanwhile, Vanessa can start looking for the Sullivans and the others—"

"Dawson," Jack stated, feeling some kind of responsibility that they didn't remain nameless.

"The Dawsons." Ivan nodded once at Jack, who did the same in recognition. "She knows how to stay out of sight." He looked at Vanessa now, as though telling her to be careful, and she half smiled. "And we can get them all out of there. Once we're done here tonight, we'll figure out something about the other problem."

"I'm going in with Mark," Jack said as a matter of fact.

"Okay, let's go!" They all headed toward the building.

"Jack, c'mon," Mark indicated that he should follow him, and the two separated from the rest of the group.

"Why are we going the other way?" Jack asked as they walked around the corner to where Mark had appeared minutes earlier.

"We have to open the door for them, and there're probably a whole bunch of Thomas's men guarding the entrance that we'll have to care of, so we gotta get in from here."

Jack would usually have questioned what they were going to do to be sure not to wind up getting *themselves* taken care of by the guards, but not now. Now nothing else mattered.

"How are we going to get in from here?" They came to a halt by a solid brick wall with no windows anywhere in reach.

"You'll see," muttered Mark, a smirk on his broad face.

Jack looked around, squinting through the many raindrops that plummeted to the ground, to see if anyone was watching them. He thought there would be more security outside Thomas's building, and it was quite a relief to see that no one but them was out here.

"Just give me a second, all right?" Mark spoke to the back of his head.

"Yeah, what are you…" He turned to face him, but Mark was gone. "I see," Jack told himself. He turned his back on the ugly building, feeling it was a better choice to stare at the darkness, looking for any sign of movement, while standing alone in the shimmering light of the only functioning street lamp, which stood a few feet away barely making a difference in the tempestuous night.

"Jack."

He spun round vigilantly when he heard his name being whispered into his ear. Mark was standing there again.

"Let's go." He gestured with his head to the drab wall.

Jack acquiesced.

Mark gripped him tightly by the elbow and pulled him. However, instead of teleporting as Jack had anticipated, Mark went *through* the wall, dragging Jack behind him. When Jack's nose was an inch from the rough surface, he felt a discomforting jolt in his stomach and waited to endure severe pain. Yet he was wrong. Passing through the hard mass of stone and cement felt nothing like pain. Instead, it felt like going into a pool of warm water with pressure closing in from every direction. It was an extremely odd experience when Jack was halfway through, with his head emerging from one side and his legs still out in the rain on the other.

When the two of them were inside Thomas's building, Mark immediately hissed, "Shhh!" and jerked his head in the direction of two men standing in front of the vast oak double doors at the entrance that they were supposed to open for the others to get inside. The men could not see Jack and Mark, as they were hiding in the shadows that were thrown upon the corridors like a thick blanket.

"We gotta knock 'em out man," Mark urged in a whisper. "There are just these two, for now." His eyes were fixed in the guards' direction yet not focused on them at all.

Nervously, Jack closed his eyes and took a deep breath. He had never used his powers for something as serious as this. He knew he needed to focus on what had to be done. And just as he was about to reopen his eyes, he felt a sudden rush of confidence flow over him. An unusual vigor began to pulse in his veins and take over him like venom. When he reopened his eyes, the colors of everything were inverted. It was as though he were looking through a heat-sensing lens. The guards' faces and hands glowed red. The rest of them, covered by coats, as well as the walls, the ceiling, and anything else that was cold, were cerulean. Jack examined his hands and then looked at Mark. Both shone crimson.

"Dude, your eyes!" Mark was taken aback.

"What?" whispered Jack, confused, looking around slowly. He saw that the shadows they were standing in were darker as opposed to where there was some source of light, giving light of a delicate scarlet shade wherever it touched.

"Jack, your eyes are…you look like you've got fire in your sockets," said Mark, enthralled.

One of the men at the door turned his head and seemed to have noticed something.

"Hey, man, stop doing that! They can see us!" Mark was urging him in a whisper that Jack could barely hear.

Not knowing how to control what was happening to him, Jack

shut his eyes tightly for a second and felt the back of his eyelids seethe. When he opened his eyes again, nothing had changed except that both of Thomas's men were merely feet away from him and Mark, treading nearer dauntingly. Jack looked at them apprehensively and turned to Mark, who was no longer there. He had no idea what to do next. He couldn't close his eyes, because that would no longer help him now that the guards were coming toward him. He was almost entirely sure that Mark hadn't fled. Nevertheless, he'd only met the guy minutes ago. He had to act fast, and there was no time to think.

Without hesitation, Jack shot a large orb of what looked like blood-red flames, aiming both hands at one of the sentries. He hit the man squarely in the chest and, as he knocked the wind out of him, there was a blur of sapphire and he hit the ground. And then, with no warning, just before the second man was about to attack Jack, two stone hands protruded from the side of the narrow corridor and pulled the man, hitting his head hard on the brick wall, knocking him out cold. The stone hand became Mark's as he stepped out of the opaque wall. It was an odd-looking sight: Mark blending into the masonry at the point where the two met, as if he had become a *part* of it.

"Nice shot," he said, breathing rapidly. "Shall we get the door?"

As they hurried to the double doors, Jack asked, "Why didn't you just get everyone in the same way you got me in?"

"I can't take more than one person at a time. And it would have been too hard for all of us to get in unnoticed—wanna do the honors?"

"My pleasure." Jack burned a hole where both locked door

handles were, and they melted away, letting the doors ease open with a soft whine.

"Finally." Eric came in first and the rest followed. He wiped his face with his hands and whispered loudly, "What took you guys so long? Wow, dude—what's up with your eyes?" He too seemed astonished by them.

"I'm not sure," Jack replied truthfully.

"Hey, Ivan," Tren said incoherently. "Look at this." He pointed at Jack's face.

Ivan came and examined Jack. "Nice…" He looked into his flaming eyes. "You're advancing fast. Have you got control over it yet?"

"No, it just…happened."

"Well, you'll get the hang of it soon enough." He spoke to everyone now, still in an undertone. "Stay alert, the place looks too empty. Thomas may be up to something."

The lot of them moved into the center of what used to be a lobby but now bore a large wooden table with many non-matching chairs; some were made of plastic, others had steel frames and moth-eaten cushions, the foam almost completely bare on most. Lying on the floor were a few empty beer bottles, and two packs of cards lay scattered on the aged wooden surface. What used to be the lobby was now a storage site for canned food and drinks.

Suddenly, gusts of pitch-black wind—bearing no features other than hollow whites for eyes, —streamed in from everywhere like glowing ribbons of smoke. Within seconds, the place was filled with blazing jets of fire and unnatural darkness whipping all around. Marisa and Allison were already gone. Jack was shooting flames anywhere he could; he did not try to strike the enemy. Rather, he focused on not hurting his friends. Ivan was lifted off his feet, and he drifted out of sight into the gloom of the higher floors. And, at that moment, Tren and Richard were dragged away too.

Thomas was definitely up to something—it was all a trap. That was why it had been so easy for them to infiltrate the building. He was waiting for them to come, so he could carry out the perfect snare. Jack turned to see if Mark was still standing. He was also taken. Jack had hit the enemy more than ten times already, but they were moving too fast and there were too many of them and he couldn't get a clear shot to put them out of motion.

Meanwhile, Eric was thrown into the air by one of them; it swiped him up and let him go so that he fell, screaming, to the floor and, with a dramatic *thud*, was silent. Now the only two left standing were Ryan and Jack. Several of the shadow-like creatures had fallen, but there were still enough to surround them. Ryan's hand darted into one that sped by him. Fire and darkness blended with each other, and a terrible high-pitched scream resounded. It was staring into Ryans's flaming blood-red eyes with its own ice-cold sockets. Then Ryan punched the thing with a blast of fire, sending it hurtling into one of the walls enclosing them. It burned back into its true human form as it took the hit. He lay in a trance, dressed in the same black attire as the other two men that guarded the door. Another one attacked Ryan, but he threw it off and the murky gale wafted above him, attempting to attack anew. But, before it could do anything, Ryan joined both his hands before him, fingers spread out, elbows glued to his sides. A beam of white-hot fire flooded from his hands, hitting the enemy while still in motion as it reformed in midair and crashed through the table. The table ended up in pieces, some still ablaze, the flames dancing wildly. Tinted glass lay, soundless and serene, on the floor. By now less than ten of Thomas's men were still skirmishing. And then they all pounded onto Ryan and Jack at once like a leopard upon prey. Ryan was the one who took most of them out. Jack had managed to take out three of them by now, but they were swirling around him like a tornado. He tried to fend them off but they worked together, and nothing he did helped. Subsequently, he heard Ryan cry out as an indigo ripple shuddered across the space, throwing off five of them. A few *thumps* sounded as they pounded to the floor.

He was breathing heavily and leaning with his hands on his knees.

"Are you okay?" Jack was concerned.

"Yeah…I'm good." He spoke quite calmly. "Let's go find them."

But just as they were about to go search for the others, another swirl of blackness entered the place. But he did not attack. He hovered a few feet above the ground, staring at Ryan intently.

"Oh, come on!" sneered Ryan. "Didn't you bastards get enough?"

Suddenly, a dim blur smeared the air, and the sleek shadow turned and gushed right through Ryan. He fell to his knees and then collapsed, shivering violently, his lips a deep purple shade, eyes batting wildly.

The attacker neared Jack and, as he began to form into his usual self, he faded to black. And before Jack stood a pale man with gray hair. He looked unusually relaxed, yet his eyes were filled with rage.

Jack looked from the man in the leather coat and assassin gloves to Ryan, who lay feeble in a dreadful condition. Jack remained rooted to the spot. The man turned his head to look at Ryan and then turned his eyes back on Jack. "Oh, don't worry about him," he said calmly, "he's just a little cold. It is pretty chilly outside." He smirked. "He'll be fine." The leer grew into a smile, and the man held out his hand. "I'm Thomas. It's a pleasure to finally meet you in person, Jack. I've heard a lot about you."

Jack didn't move.

Thomas withdrew his handshake. "That's okay, we have got much to talk about." Unexpectedly, he placed his hand on Jack's forehead and, before Jack could do anything about it, he watched everything fade to black.

***

"Morning, sleeping beauty," said Thomas lightheartedly as Jack slid his eyes open and got up from the carpeted floor. He was standing in a small office with gray walls. In the center of the room stood a sturdy aluminum desk with a chair at either side. Thomas was seated behind it. "Have a seat." He gestured to the empty chair opposite him.

Silently, Jack drew back the chair and, while doing so, saw a silver key threaded onto a necklace tangled around Thomas's fingers. He felt for the necklace that was supposed to be around his neck, but there was only a thin scratch where it had been pried from him while he was unconscious. He sat down, keeping his eyes half closed because even the faint florescent light that was mounted on the wall behind Thomas was too bright with the headache he had .Being knocked out in some magical way was extremely unpleasant.

"You're probably wondering why I'm doing all of this. Why I'm causing so much trouble for everyone," Thomas began.

"Because of your greed for more power?" Jack replied rhetorically.

"Not quite," continued Thomas serenely. "Let me tell you how this all started, thirty years ago… Have you heard of Michael Xelticus?"

"I have," said Jack coldly.

"Good, then you know about the eight members and the stone?"

Jack merely looked at him while he was talking. He felt hatred flow in his blood like a poison. Nevertheless, he remained silent and didn't try to escape, because he was sure that he did not have the slightest chance of doing so. Thomas was more powerful than anyone he had seen until now. Nonetheless, despite how much he despised him, Jack couldn't help but wonder why Thomas's abilities were so different from the other members of Xelticus. Ivan had definitely told him that they all shared the same ability. Despite his curiosity, Jack listened impatiently since all he cared about was finding out what had happened to Claire and his parents and Kyle and Jessica and his friends, and this man had the answer. He yearned to ask where they were.

"Michael's son, Nich—" Thomas began.

"Where are they?" Jack interrupted him. "Where's my family and my friends? What have you done with them?"

Thomas sighed impatiently. "They're fine. I didn't hurt anyone.

In fact, the whole bunch is in Italy. They are on their way there, right now, as we speak. Now we…" He looked down at his watch. "Have got to leave on the eight o'clock flight." He looked back at Jack. "It's two a.m. right now, but don't worry. That's more than enough time for me to finish telling you *my* story." He sighed again when he saw how uninterested Jack was in his tale.

"When I finish telling you this, you'll understand why I'm doing all of this."

Jack still remained silent.

"As I was saying, Nicholas was Michael Xelticus's son… It was a Sunday night, and Michael and his wife had been preparing a surprise party for Nicholas since that morning, when he left the house. They made sure that he spent the entire day with his friends so that night…" He paused for a moment. "When it was time for the party, Michael gave me a call and asked me if I could pick up Nicholas and bring him home. You see, I was his favorite Uncle Tom, and he was really excited that I was coming to visit him on his birthday. So… I went and fetched Nicholas from his friend's house."

Thomas's eyes were suddenly filled with sadness, though he seemed to be ignoring what he felt.

"On the way home," he continued in a lower voice, "we were talking about all the things that Nick wanted to do now that he was eight years old." He half laughed. "We had this little joke that his label changed every year from 'baby' to 'man.' On his eighth birthday, he had grown from 'little boy' to 'boy.'" Thomas laughed again. Now he couldn't hide the sorrow but proceeded as though it didn't exist.

"When we were only one block away from his house,

somehow…I…lost control of the car. Some drunk bastard came flying down the road at full speed. I pressed my foot on the brake and held the horn down flat. But, unfortunately, it was too late for either of us to stop." He paused again, took a deep breath, and resumed. "At the moment of the collision, I tried to throw myself onto Nicholas, but my damn seatbelt held me back — ironic isn't it?. I couldn't move. It was no use—he died on the spot. I couldn't save him."

"I'm sorry." Jack had not planned on saying this, but he deemed it heartless not to. Besides, now he no longer felt the same hatred that he had before. Still, he hated Thomas for kidnapping the people that he loved.

"Obviously, I blamed myself. It was my fault. I didn't know how I was supposed to live with myself after that. And I couldn't bear the thought that I would eventually have to look his parents in the eye. When they found out what happened, well…his mother got so sick that she became bedridden. Earlier that year, she had been diagnosed with cancer—she had only three years left. And knowing that she would not spend them with her son…it killed her faster.

"As for Michael, he didn't even want to hear about me. What could you expect, huh?" Now his face was weighed down with anger as well.

"And then he called me the night after the funeral…said I must come to his office, it was in his house, and his wife didn't know I was there—she wouldn't have been able to handle it. So I did. I went. When I got there, the front door was unlocked, like he said it would be, and I let myself in quietly. It felt like no one had lived in the damn place for years. And the family's caretaker, Zachary, directed me to the office.

"When I went in, Michael told me to stay standing, even though I wouldn't have sat down anyway. Hell, I tried talking to the man, but he didn't want to listen. He just shut me up and ordered me to give him my coin. And I obeyed. I thought he was going to kick me out of the Xelticus group, and I accepted it wholeheartedly. But oh no..."

Now hate lingered in his eyes. "He did something so much worse—worse than killing me," he said indignantly, his voice rising.

"Michael took my coin, pushed me against the wall, and held it right here..." He pointed to his chest. "Against my heart. He asked me how I felt, and I told him. I said I felt sad, bitter, angry, felt like I was locked inside some dark cell, trapped within myself, that I couldn't sleep at night. And...I have no idea how the hell he did it, but the coin lit up. It was a bright yellow light, and an unreal warmth washed over me. And it suddenly became solid as ice... I thought I had been frozen to the core. I started screaming, but my throat was so dry that nothing came out." Thomas took a deep breath, his cold eyes looking deadly and dangerous.

"Then it stopped. It was horrible." He stopped talking and stood up.

"That's how I became like this. I feel the same way I felt then, every single second of every single day. I can't sleep, and anything I eat or drink tastes as bitter as gall." He yelled the last few words then stared at Jack for a few uncomfortable moments, biting his lip. His eyes were on the verge of overflowing with tears of despair. He blinked and stood up straight, fixing his coat firmly on his shoulders. "You know..." he said quietly, almost in a whisper. "You'd think that I've got nothing to live for, but I still have a kid.

She's all grown up now. I had to raise her myself, and a short while after this incident with Nicholas, her mother died in a car crash. She's worth living and dying for, and now she doesn't even speak to me because of what I've become. But...*if*... No..." He waved his finger in the air and chuckled. "*When* I get my hands on that stone, I believe that the power it holds is strong enough to break this curse, or whatever it is that Michael Xelticus did to me. I can't be dead inside anymore."

Thomas took the key he had placed on the desk while he was talking and put it safely inside his coat. He walked to the door and opened it. "You may want to get some sleep, kid. We're going to Italy tomorrow, and we've got to leave for the flight in four hours." He stood with his back turned to Jack, who was still seated, speaking as though nothing had just happened.

"You have the coins, why do you need me or my family? Just go get the damn rock and leave us out of this," said Jack indignantly.

"Haven't they told you?" Thomas turned to face Jack again.

Jack said nothing.

"I need all of you there," started Thomas, "because I need you Jack. I need your blood. Have you heard the term New Blood?"

"Yes."

"Good. When you touched that coin, it became yours. And now I need your blood to open the door to the stone because your blood is not in the mixture that was used to create those horrid coins." A smile spread across Thomas's face when he saw the fretfulness on Jack. "Don't worry, Jack, I don't need all of it. But I do need it fresh if it's going to work, so you're going to have to join me I'm afraid."

"And the others, why take them?" demanded Jack, privately

relieved to know that Thomas did not intend to spill his blood on that door.

"I want them to see." Thomas's eyes flashed bright white and returned to normal, an impish on his pale face. "To see who I really am."

"Who cares?" at once Jack knew that this question was a mistake.

Thomas flew toward Jack in a gust of blackness and towered over him. From the strain on his face Jack could see that it took everything in the man to prevent himself from ripping Jack apart that very moment. And then Thomas spoke very slowly: "For— my—daughter." Thomas backed away,

"Ah, Brian!" Someone had just come up the stairs. The newcomer's face was covered by a beard and a cap that almost covered his eyes. "Keep an eye on him, will you?" Thomas patted him twice on the shoulder and hurried down the steep flight of stairs.

Brian reached from the outside of the room and, without a word, closed the door. Jack heard it being locked from the other side. He turned off the light, got on the floor, and lay on his back, staring at the low ceiling above. He was looking forward to going to Italy. Of course the only reason was that he would finally get to see his family again. He missed his mother's dominance and his father's agreeing with her. He missed Kyle and Jessy arguing with each other about stupid things, like which of them got the front seat of the car, and then making jokes about it. He missed Claire's smile… He missed everything about Claire.

At least he knew that they were safe and unhurt. Somehow he

knew that Thomas hadn't lied about that (or anything else for that matter), just as Vanessa and Ivan had assured him, "Thomas would never do something like that." Jack knew that he would not get any sleep if he tried, and he needed it. Hence, he just lay there and ignited both hands, leaning on his elbows on the dusty floor, and watched the red light dance unceremoniously over him, picturing Claire's features in the shifting shadows

- CHAPTER EIGHT -
IL L'ARCO

Jack awoke the next morning with a seatbelt around his waist in an uncomfortable seat. The bright sunlight flowed serenely into the airplane through the small window beside him. His head was heavy; it felt like a large golf ball was mounted on his neck. Drowsiness drowned him, and a stinging pain thumped in his left shoulder. He felt a small bump under his black T-shirt, and he lifted the sleeve to take a look.

"Oh, yeah, we gave you a sedative," said Thomas lightly when he saw Jack examining the injection wound.

Jack threw him a look of great dislike. Only now he realized Thomas was sitting next to him. He may have felt slight pity for him after hearing his depressing story, but he was still as resentful as ever toward Thomas.

"I just thought we'd rather be safe than sorry," Thomas explained calmly, though Jack did not think that this man had to explain himself when he did deviant things.

Thomas was not looking at Jack, but he continued to speak to him. "We're going to land in about five hours; we took an earlier flight than expected. We're going from the airport directly to *Il L'Arco*. That is the tourist site where the stone is. I've got a few friends working on the inside there, so the place has been off limits for the past two weeks—'construction problems'—so the place will be quite empty. And to avoid any attention at all, we are going to initiate the entire plan at night. Your family and friends are already there, Jack."

And for the remaining few hours of the flight, Jack sat with headphones covering his ears and stared out the square window at the horizon as it transformed from a peaceful azure into indigo.

***

"You'll never get away with this!" Ivan was yelling at the top of his lungs. He was half-leaning on the rough, jagged stone wall behind him while struggling to break free from the chains that were binding his arms behind his back. "I won't let it!"

"Oh, really? What are you going to do about it?" retorted Max from the end of the dark spherical chamber. He was standing by the arched entrance, which was only about an inch taller than he was. "You are useless now! All of you!" He laughed hysterically and waved his arms, gesturing to the rest of the people trapped inside there. The Sullivan family, Claire and her parents, Tren with his wife and Mark and Ryan, who seemed to be lifeless. Pale like a ghost, he lay motionless, bound by chains like the others. Every now and then, he shuddered as though signaling that he was not dead. At least not yet.

"You cannot destroy those shackles with fire. None of you with that ability are strong enough, not even if you can go as far as red flames! I made sure of that myself. You know, at first I was worried about Ryan over there, but he will definitely not be a problem," Max mocked cruelly. "I'm going to leave you fellas alone. Spend some quality time together. Get to know each other better!" He laughed coldly again and walked out through the curved doorway, sealing it with a heavy stone door. Grinding noise screamed in their ears as total darkness grew upon them. First there was dead silence for a few moments; then Claire spoke for the first time since she had been captured.

"What was he talking about?" She breathed shakily. "The fire…"

"I don't know, sweetie," replied her mother through tears of fear, although she was somewhat joyful that her daughter had spoken after so many weeks of keeping silent in shock. Besides, there was not much to talk about.

All they could see were silhouettes (and barely that), as the only source of light was a sliver of light through a slender crack from where the boulder door was not sealed completely.

"Let's just be grateful that we are still alive," her father said in a deep voice. "I knew that that *Jack* kid was trouble from the start!" he added indignantly. "You think it's a coincidence that his *whole* family is—"

"Hey!" Kyle's voice ricocheted. For a second, there was a blue flash followed by the sound of metal clanking onto the mildewed floor and ringing in the stuffy, stifling air. Suddenly, as though a torch had been lit, flames flickered in front of Claire and her parents. Her mother and father gasped at the sight of Kyle's burning fist being the source of sapphire light. Claire, on the other hand, was surprised yet not as taken aback as her parents.

Jack's brother was face to face with George Dawson. "Don't even *think* about blaming my brother for this!" he said through gritted teeth. "He didn't even know what the hell was happening to him when all this started. He didn't choose this, and he definitely had no idea of the danger he was in."

"The danger *he* was in?" said Mr. Dawson haughtily. He seemed to have forgotten Kyle's blazing hand.

"*OR* the danger that anyone close to him was in, because we are dealing with psychopaths!" Kyle stood up and took a deep breath, still looking at the mesmerized Dawsons. Claire's mother was hugging her tightly as though to serve as a shield if anything were to go wrong.

"What the hell is this!?" insisted Mr. Dawson, stupefied.

"There are people who have special abilities, and those guys out there are only one step away from getting their hands on something dangerous."

"A weapon?" asked Mr. Dawson with apprehension.

"Yeah," said Kyle tersely. "But listen…" He turned his back on them and spoke to the others as he walked to Ryan. "If we want to get out of here, we're going to have to work together. We'll get you unchained, and we must stick together and put an end to all of this."

"I'm so proud of him," Sarah whispered to Ben, glowing with pride, a small smile on her face.

Kyle placed his hand on Ryan's forehead and shut his eyes in concentration. A blue sheet of radiance covered Ryan's entire body, seeping onto his hands from under his sleeves. His face filled with color as the energy pulsated through him. Immediately he rose as the chains broke off with ease.

"Thanks, man."

Both of them freed the others, leaving Mr. Dawson for last. "Oh, that's nice," he said cynically when he was the last one still sitting.

"Oh, no hard feelings, man!" said Kyle with a radiant smile as he removed Mr. Dawson's shackles and helped him up. George nodded frantically and rubbed his wrists. When they were all standing in one group, Kyle announced, "Let's do this!"

***

A loud scream of engines echoed in the cold night as the plane glided out of the sky and onto the misty runway. Like an enormous hawk, it prowled upon the tarmac in the thick darkness as it slowly came to a halt.

"We're here," announced Thomas, unbuckling the belt. "Get up, kid, we've got lots to do!" He stood motionless and waited for Jack.

When Jack got out of the chair, he discovered that the plane was almost completely empty. The people that sat in front of him, behind him, and to the side all worked for Thomas. They had blocked any view beyond themselves until now; Jack had not even gotten up to use the bathroom. He also saw that the plane was a small one. Even so, it was too empty.

Chilled air filled Jack's nostrils the moment he stepped outside. Smoky mist besieged him, creating a calm atmosphere even though tension was all that seemed to exist of late. Three jet black Jeeps with tinted windows and no license plates were parked in front of a rather small airport. It was old fashioned, and the beige paint was peeling off the low building's walls. Water stains ran to the ground in dirty trails from the few broken gutters that lined the roof of the unkempt structure. Yet, even though it was not in good shape, it still looked like an expensive work of art.

As they approached the awaiting cars, a tall man with a large, square build stepped out of the driver's seat of the foremost vehicle and opened the back door for Thomas, who had instructed Jack, when they were still in the air, to follow him. Jack hated receiving orders from him. But this was the only smart thing to do unless he wanted to end up like Ryan—if he was still alive. An extremely uncomfortable knot jolted in Jack's stomach at the thought that Ryan might be dead. It was like having a baseball thrust into his gut with great force. And the very thought of standing side by side with the person responsible was unnerving.

"We are going straight to *Il L'Arco*, aren't we?" Thomas said to the muscular man.

"Yeah, I've taken care of everything," Max replied shortly in a deep voice. Jack saw much dislike for Thomas in Max's stone-cold eyes. Thomas had clearly decided to ignore this matter, as he was obviously aware of this. Thomas gave a fake smile and gestured for Jack to enter before him. Max stooped and returned to the driver's seat, the moon's pale light reflecting on his bald head as it filtered through the mist. The three engines rumbled nearly simultaneously and set off.

The ride to the tourist site at which the stone was kept was long and nerve-racking. Almost soundlessly, the bulky cars glided along the paved and creviced streets of Italy. Squat buildings and stalls flashed by, darkness cloaking the flat rooftops.

At last, after what seemed to be ten hours of sheer frustration, the road stopped being swiped from underneath them and they came to a halt. Thomas opened the door, stepped outside, and waited for Jack. As soon as the door was slammed shut behind them, the Jeep drove away accompanied by the other two. Now Thomas and Jack were the only ones standing in front of *Il L'Arco*. A vast arched doorway gave entrance to the magnificent cave. Thomas gripped Jack by the arm and led the way inside, past the taped off entrance and danger and construction signs, not speaking a single word. Thomas's face was radiant with avarice and anticipation, a rather crazy look glowing in his eyes. He was as serious as ever. He did not even blink.

Torches illuminated the old, tunnel-like passageways. Carvings similar to hieroglyphics, yet different in an unusual way, lined the sides of the low-ceilinged stone maze. Every now and then, Thomas would turn sharply to the right or left, passing through passages that looked identical to previously visited ones, making Jack feel as though they were tracking in circles. Thomas, on the other hand, knew exactly where he was going.

And after many twists and turns, they came to a dead end. Nevertheless, Jack saw something that made his heart leap. On the stone wall before him was something familiar. Something he hadn't seen in quite a while. Something that was the keystone of so much confusion and the source of everything that had happened lately. This was the beginning of all the events that had occurred since his birthday, a lifetime ago. And now…this was the end.

- CHAPTER NINE -

THE END

Emerging from the rough rock was a smooth, eight-armed star. Etched across its heart was the word *XELTICUS*. Near the vertex between each of the sharp-edged points were eight spherical depressions with a star in the center. A much smaller star, yet identical to the one they surrounded.

"Here it is," said Thomas after a long silence spent staring at the symbol. He finally released Jack's arm. "Just like we left it twenty-nine years ago." He seemed somewhat relieved at the sight. After another moment or so, he tore his eyes from the stone wall, reached inside his coat, and pulled out a small leather pouch that jingled. The clinking sound was so soft, almost unheard, the flaming torches mounted alongside them licking at the dark serenely. Thomas loosened the thread and, with two fingers, extracted a coin (the exact same coin Jack had gotten from Kyle on his birthday) and placed it in the circular depression at the bottom left corner. As he did, a hollow grinding noise sounded from within—it was like a gear cogging into place.

Thomas did this with another five coins, placing each in a

specific spot, until the pouch was empty. He let it drop, and a little puff of dust rose when it hit the cracked floor. He then turned to face Jack and held out his hand. Jack looked at his open palm and at once knew what Thomas wanted. Jack felt in his pocket for his own coin and gave it to Thomas, who immediately turned his back on Jack and placed the shiny silver disk in the top right niche. Now there was only one open spot left, directly beneath Jack's coin. (He reckoned that it must have been his father's spot when Xelticus was formed.) Again, Thomas reached into his coat and carefully added his own coin in the designated spot. Thomas's coin did not have a bright appearance like the others. It looked dull, as though it were dead. And then Jack remembered how every one of the eight members had used a drop of their own blood when they had forged the coins. There was clearly some sort of connection between the coin and its master. When the grinding noise was heard once again, Jack expected something to happen, maybe a bit of shuddering beneath their feet and sand falling from above their heads.

Nothing happened.

"There's just one last piece to the puzzle," said Thomas in a low hiss. His eyes were on Jack, who suddenly had the impression that a snake was staring at him. Jack looked back but remained silent.

And then, without any warning whatsoever, Thomas slashed a gash in Jack's right shoulder with a sharp dagger. Jack screamed. It felt as though the blade was white-hot when it pierced his flesh. Instinctively, he clutched the wound with his other hand.

"What the hell are you doing!?" panted Jack, crouched over the small puddle of blood that was forming at his feet. "You're crazy!"

"Yeah, well…" said Thomas carelessly. "You would be too…" He was holding the bloody dagger, facing down, before his eyes, watching the thick red liquid dribble and drip off. "If you had gone through what I have." He turned his back again.

Jack felt the warm blood rushing through his fingers and began to feel slightly lightheaded and weak.

"I'm sorry that it had to come to this, although I must say, Jack," Thomas continued and paced toward the emblem. "I have a damn good reason for everything I do." He suddenly stabbed Jack's coin. It was resting in the dent, so the blade did not penetrate the silver. A blinding white light burst out as the two metals met. Each one of the other coins lit up simultaneously after that, and Thomas dropped the dagger with a clatter and backed away, his arms covering his face. Jack bowed his head and shut his eyes to see the back of his eyelids glow red. A warm wave slowly swept over them, impairing their hearing. But it did something else as well, something like no other experience he had undergone. While still clutching the deep gouge in his shoulder, Jack felt the open skin rejoin with itself and seal. The bleeding stopped, and the wave flushed over him, leaving everything the way it had been a few seconds before, except for the dead end where they were standing. Jack stood up straight and saw that the wall had edged back. He felt strong and healthy again. His lesion was completely healed, as though it had never been there to start with.

Thomas let out a mad laugh. His eyes were wide with joy. "You see, Jack?" he said radiantly. "It healed you. Maybe it can help me!" He prodded his chest repeatedly as he spoke, staring at Jack, full of excitement. "Come on!"

Thomas was suddenly behaving like a like a child about to get a mountain bike for his birthday. And, seemingly, he wanted to share his excitement with Jack, as if they were best friends.

"You know why I needed your blood?" asked Thomas.

Jack was bewildered by Thomas's sudden change of personality. "You told me the coin was mine and you needed my blood because it wasn't in the mixture," he replied, remembering his conversation with Thomas.

"Well, not exactly…" Thomas was struggling to push the heavy stone door. "I'm sure you heard the story of your birth—give me hand!"

Jack, one step behind him, obeyed, still rather confused by this.

"When your heart was weak?" he continued.

"Yeah," said Jack as the two succeeded in pushing the slab of rock to reveal an opening to their right.

"Well, Ben took his coin…" Thomas hurriedly walked back into the passage and took a torch out of its bracket "And he used that and the stone to heal you. All he needed to do was put the coin together with the stone for a while so it would absorb as much of the power as possible. Michael had my coin at the time, so they used it to get—of course I wouldn't have prevented Ben from getting help for his son…"

"And?" They were now walking in a square tunnel, narrower than the ones they had been through earlier. Jack, eager to hear the answer to his question, was still one step behind Thomas.

He continued, slightly out of breath. "When your dad brought the coin to the hospital, he put it against your heart…" They took a sharp turn to the left, the orange flame flickering uncomfortably.

"And you healed. But somehow, after that, you became a part of the Xelticus group." They were practically jogging. "And the door can only be opened with every single member's coin. And since your coin doesn't have your blood, I had to add it." Thomas came to a sudden stop in front of another dead end. "I had to use your blood because of that."

The two were breathing heavily in the oxygen-deprived space. Jack felt his heart throbbing in his throat, sweat swathing him. "What now?"

"Hold on." Thomas threw the torch aside and placed both hands on the wall before him. Jack watched in astonishment and as it froze and turned pale, almost white. Icy air could be seen rising from it, and there was a light crackle. The torch's flame began to die out.

"Do your thing, kid. Blow it away," said Thomas excitedly, staring at the frozen wall. Jack hesitated; he had almost forgotten what Thomas was.

And as though Thomas could hear Jack's thoughts, he said, "I'm not what you think I am." He looked at Jack now. "I just want to live again, Jack," he said sincerely, his eyes filled with sorrow. "I don't want more power. I never did. I just want to feel again."

Jack looked at him for a moment. "What about Ryan?" he said at once.

"He's fine—but honestly, do you think he would have listened if I'd tried explaining this to him? This is my one chance."

Jack stood still. The torch on the floor was as dim as a matchstick by now.

"Please."

Jack considered and then faced the cold slab. The light

shimmered and went out.

Red flames ripped through the pitch-black space and clashed with the sturdy stone. It exploded with a loud *bang*, and light filtered through the settling dust. But it was not a regular glow. It was an electric blue that brightly illuminated the small room beyond the hole that Jack had just blown open.

Mounted on a low rock in the center was a transparent box with metallic rims for a skeleton. The stone that lay inside was misshapen like any other and was as large as a fist. Nevertheless, its nature was unlike anything else Jack had ever seen. It was radiant and beautiful. It looked peaceful, yet powerful, sending ripples of energy through the room as though it was beating like a heart. It was simply astounding.

Thomas carefully picked up the glass case and spoke with his back to Jack. "Follow me."

He led him back out into the torch-lit corridors. Only this time, he walked more slowly, keeping his eyes on the stone and looking up every now and then to make sure that he would not bump into any walls. Jack was striding frantically a few paces behind him with mixed feelings.

He was excited that he would finally be able to reunite with Claire and his family. He missed them all so much. And he also wanted to see Vanessa and Eric and the others. He was worrying about them. He wanted to be sure that they were all right. He was also extremely relieved that this whole mess would come to an end at last. No more looking over his shoulder and worrying about loved ones being constantly in danger's spotlight. No more fighting and no more hatred. Just peace. Things would finally go back to the way they used to be. Maybe not *exactly* the same, but it was just as good.

On the other hand, Jack could not relax not knowing whether helping Thomas was the right choice or not. After all, this man had not proven himself trustworthy at all. But even so, he couldn't help but realize that Thomas would have no reason for lying about the past. He did not entirely follow his logic for his decision and was hoping fervently that it would not come back and haunt him with grave consequences. Now all he could do was wait anxiously and find out.

"Where are we going?" he asked Thomas after walking for five minutes or so.

"To your family and friends," replied Thomas.

Jack's heart leaped with joy and excitement; he had been waiting for this for so long.

"I want them to see this when it happens…to show them I haven't changed into what they think I have become." He continued walking straight and then turned right, carefully clutching the stone in his hand. "Especially Ivan and…" he sighed. They were now heading up a flight of stairs that rose to some place out of sight.

"Why him?" asked Jack.

"He hasn't told you?" said Thomas with a slight laugh, still watching the stone—more carefully now that they were climbing sandy old stairs. "Well…I've got my reasons."

At the head of the stairs, Thomas asked Jack to push the wall that stood in front of them, and it wheeled open to reveal an opening similar to the previous one. But this passage was to an ancient chamber, illuminated by torches that surrounded them. In each of the four corners was a large copper plate emblazoned with flames, giving the place a vivacious glow. Jack and Thomas walked in through one of the corners, and Jack felt the heat from the brass platter over his head beat on the back of his neck as he walked underneath it. The chamber held a vast stone edifice in the shape of a temple. Its three walls rose about ten feet over their heads. Stairs led up the fissured construction facing the entrance to the chamber, which was big enough to fit an industrial container.

"Come with me." Thomas headed up this second set of steps, eyes still fixed on the radiant stone.

The wall reached just a little above his waist at the flat-bottomed top. And, in the center of the open space, there was a large pale rock wrought roughly like a cube. It was level with the enveloping boundary with a ragged surface. Thomas gently placed the glass case on it. Once again he reached into his coat. This time he took something that Jack recognized well and brought back a flash of the odd dream he'd had quite a while ago. Thomas placed the silver key into the slot on the rim of the stone's enclosure and turned it slowly. The chain that was threaded on the key slid and rattled softly as it came to a rest at Thomas's feet.

"Couldn't you just break the glass?" asked Jack, remembering how Vanessa had gone through all that trouble to ensure that the key was well protected.

"As long as the stone is in here, the glass is stronger than bulletproof," replied Thomas shortly, focused on opening the lid. "Just a drop in the sea of the power that it holds…" he murmured.

Then Jack understood that Thomas only treated the stone with such great care because he admired it so much.

He turned the box around and opened a second lock, on the opposite side, that Jack had not noticed before. Thomas lifted the lid and placed it aside. He rested his hands on either side of the mouth of the transparent box, eyes wide open, full of glee and hope. A faint smile could be seen on his face.

"THOMAS DON'T!" Ivan's voice echoed loudly. He had just come running into the chamber. Moments later, Jack's heart took a dive, and warmth spread inside his chest. Claire entered, looking alert, turning her head right and left to see who was in there. She looked just as beautiful as always. Her long hair draped like a curtain, covering the side of her dazzling face, the torchlight glimmering in her striking blue eyes.

"Jack, get down there!" yelled Ivan from the foot of the stairs.

Only when she heard his name did Claire's face light up, and she looked up to see Jack. They gazed into each other's eyes. Jack was about to run down the stairs to her when, suddenly, a black gust of wind swooped in swiftly, spreading gloom and darkness in the chamber. It was followed by the rest of the Sullivans, Claire's parents, a drowsy Mark leaning on his father's shoulder, with his mother beside him, and Eric, who was carrying an unconscious Vanessa in his arms. Then Jack saw something he was not expecting. Kyle was standing at the tail of the group with Ryan, his hands slightly apart at his sides, blazing with crimson flames from the shoulder down, licking the air like whips.

A chill prickled at the back of Jack's neck as a black stream of cold (and somewhat evil) air passed close behind him. It flowed like water to a spot beside Thomas and formed into a man. Max eyed the stone and turned bloodshot eyes, full of greed, to Thomas.

"They managed to escape. They got out while I was in the airport with you," said Max haughtily. "I got here too late to stop them." He was talking about them with so much hatred, as if he were superior to everyone else in the room, including Thomas. Yet it was as though Thomas had sworn his allegiance to Max and—therefore, seemingly with a tremendous effort—spoke with some sort of respect.

"It's all right, Max, I wanted them all to be here to see this happen," Thomas told him serenely. He turned to the others and looked at Ivan as he spoke. "I'm finally going to put an end to this hell that I've been living until now. And everyone that has helped me will get their reward as I have promised—like I said, *I'm a man of my word.*"

"You don't have to do this," said Ivan.

"YES I DO!" retorted Thomas.

"NO!" Ivan's eyes were filled with the same sadness Jack had seen before when Thomas was mentioned. "The stone will not help you! Nothing and no one can help you other than yourself! Michael didn't want to punish you, to make you suffer! He was your best friend."

Thomas was staring at Ivan, dazed and livid.

"He was helping you. He knew that you would never forgive yourself for Nicholas's death."

Thomas clenched his jaw, and his eyes glittered with tears instantly. "*This* is help?"

"It isn't a curse," Ivan said anxiously, smiling faintly. "This is…" He paused and moved his eyes as though in search of the words to say. "A blessing. As soon as *you* stop blaming yourself for what happened that night—when you accept the fact that it was not *your* fault, that it was fate. There was nothing in the world that you could have done to prevent it. When you stop feeling guilty, only then you will be free. All this pain and suffering will come to an end. All this *hell* will be over… I tried to tell you—we all did—but you just left. You didn't want to listen."

The two stared at each other for a few silent moments, ignoring everyone around them who were watching intently.

"All you have to do is forgive yourself."

Thomas stared into space for a while and then lowered his head to stare at his feet; a tear dripped from his eye and fell on the floor. He blinked and looked up, raising his hand a little to look at it, and fanned out his fingers slightly, as though holding the air.

And then, pitch-black flames emerged from his hand and blended into a bright orange color as they rose and whispered in the silence. Thomas swallowed. He started laughing with a sense of liberation. Ivan too smiled with relief. Happiness let itself loose into the environment. Every single soul in the room was content; some showed it more than others. The "war" was over at last; all the horrid darkness had finally come to an end.

All were jovial except for one. Nobody except for Max saw the sparks that sputtered in his hands for a moment. "You got me where I wanted, I don't need you anymore Thomas," smirked Max wickedly.

And then, with no warning whatsoever, a white electric current exploded with a flash like lightning, sending Thomas hurtling down the crude stairs. He landed on his back with a *crash*.

"THOMAS!" screamed Ivan in despair. He sprinted the short

distance. Jack also ran down the stairs and stood by Thomas in shock, not knowing what to do.

Ivan was on his knees supporting Thomas's head with his arms. Thomas took hold of Ivan's hand and opened his mouth to speak.

"I love you, brother," breathed Thomas heavily. And the realization hit Jack with a blow.

"I love you too, little man." Ivan let out a weak laugh through his swollen eyes and streaming tears. Sniffing repeatedly.

"Tell Vanessa…" Thomas paused and struggled to take a deep breath then continued. "I am *so* proud of her…" He struggled again. "More than she can imagine. And…her mother is, too."

"I will." Ivan could not control his tears anymore. "I…I promise," he choked.

Thomas smiled and held his last breath. Slowly, he slid his eyes closed and lay still in his brother's arms.

"No…no…no…don't leave me, not now!" Ivan shook his brother, desperate for hope; however, it was nowhere to be found. "Come on! Come on, damn it! Breathe!" He dropped his head onto Thomas's chest and cried like a baby. "C'mon!" His voice was muffled once more, and he hit the floor hard with his fist.

Jack choked on the verge of tears when a dramatic buzzing, static noise erupted from the top of the stairs. He looked up and saw that Max was clutching the stone in his hand. Immense amounts of energy, dazzling like northern lights, were flowing fast from the stone into Max. His mouth was open as though he were screaming in great pain. His face was screwed up and his eyes tightly shut. Max's entire body was being blasted by blinding bright light. Ribbons of it whipped into the air, now in various colors like violent and green ripples in a pond. Suddenly, he opened his eyes wide. They issued the same light, like powerful torches in murky water, and beams spurted from his sockets. And then it all stopped. Max looked just as he had before. Only now an evil smile sprawled across his beastly face, eyes shining like a bloodhound.

Carelessly, he dropped the stone back into the glass shell with a crack. The stone was no longer unique. Now it was just a dull, gray rock. As though it had died, just like Thomas.

Before anyone could do anything, Max raised both arms and a powerful wave of ice cold force stretched out before him, knocking out anyone in its path.. Jack ducked just in time so that his head was missed by less than an inch, and he felt a frosty wind sweep over his short hair. He saw Mr. Dawson pull his wife and daughter down, avoiding it as well. Ivan was still on his knees, weeping, not caring—or knowing for that matter—of the imminent chaos. Only those who had managed to avoid the attack were awake now.

"It's good to be back. I still gotta get the hang of all this power." Max turned his ugly face on Jack, who had just returned to his feet. "I'm going to enjoy this," muttered Max.

Jack watched him as he neared slowly.

"There's just one last piece to the puzzle." Max edged down the dirty stairs. "In order for me…" He raised a hand to his chest. "To be able to push the boundaries to the utmost, I must possess *every single bit* of the stone's *wonderful* power." He was looking Jack in the eye with a relentless smirk.

Jack did not back away; he stood sturdily rooted to the spot.

"One…last…drop…of…blood." He mouthed each word as

he flounced the last few steps until he was face to face with Jack, towering over him. The smirk was filled with loathing, and Max said curtly, "I'm going to kill you."

Before Jack's fear could surface, he heard Claire scream, "NO!"

"QUIET!" roared Max suddenly. Heartlessly, without so much as looking at her, he threw his arm in Claire's direction and knocked her onto her back with a jet stream of lashing electricity. Mrs. Dawson yowled and ran to her daughter, who lay still on her back upon the unpleasantly cold stone floor.

"So that's why Thomas brought *her* here... I was wondering about that — see your family and all these people from the past made sense..." Max thought aloud. "But these random people... Now it makes sense. True love. Your heart belongs to her and that power is ... immense." Max smiled evilly, "happy accident for me..."

Jack was in shock, eyes wide open with horror. He could not breathe. His heart just stopped beating. Max grabbed him tightly by his throat. With incredible ease, he lifted Jack off his feet. "Your turn," he articulated through gritted teeth. Jack was choking. He could not turn his head but twisted his eyes as much as they would give.

Claire still hadn't moved. Both her parents were panicking right there next to her, holding her, calling her, shaking her.

All the blood in Jack's body rushed to his head, and anger burned deadlier than a furnace inside—like a volcano about to erupt. He shut his eyes and opened them again to look at Max, who narrowed his eyes.

Jack could feel the blue flames blaze in his sockets, spread in his skull, and bleed through his entire body. He felt the hatred pump in his veins, overshadowing all trepidation that existed.

When the electric blue inferno ruptured, so much heat billowed to Max that he flew backward with a violent jerk and smashed into the staircase, creating a crater-like ditch, dust forming itself into a cloud.

"You've got some fight in you—I like that."

But Jack was not listening. He had already come to Max and started beating him with flaming fists. A blinding flash exploded with every cracking hit. He punched as hard as he could, and pushed all his strength as far as it would take him. No remorse whatsoever. He hit him, again and again, in the face. Laughing madly, not even a scratch on his sordid face, Max caught Jack's fist.

"That's enough." He blasted Jack backward. His shoulder scraped the floor as he skidded. Max straightened up and so did Jack—as much as he could—clutching his abrasions, which throbbed with pain, and breathing heavily, the taste of blood in his mouth.

"I've had it with you."

"Bring it on!" exhaled Jack, glowering at him.

Max laughed indignantly. "Don't you understand?" He was seemingly slithering toward Jack, who didn't care what would happen next. He would fight to the death if that was what it took, but he would do all that he could to give this monster what he deserved.

Before he could get to Jack, both Kyle and his father came between the two. "Back away!" warned Ben. For the first time Jack saw both his brother and his father using their abilities. Flames in their palms at the ready. Green flames in Ben's hands, blue in Kyle's. Just like Jack, the most powerful kind.

"No!" Jack struggled but couldn't get to his feet, not just yet, so he slumped back down on his elbow.

"Smart kid, knows I'll kill you too. Just like I did his girl." Max smiled.

"We'll have to see about that," spat Kyle.

Saying nothing Max raised his left hand, both Kyle and Ben attacked him but it was useless. An electric shield deflected the flames and sent them flying across the chamber and smashing into the stone walls. With a wave of his hands Max sent a shockwave that knocked both Jack's brother and Father off their feet and anyone else who was standing in the chamber. Even Jack, who was still recovering on the ground, got flattened by the force. And he saw that wretched stone a few inches from his face. The stone that gave Max all this power. Utterly useless.

Now Max clutched Ben and Kyle by their throats and picked them up like two ragdolls. "I'm going to roast you." "No..." whispered Jack.

"Only God can stop me now!" screamed Max.

The horrible sizzling electric noise began to buzz but stopped when Max unexpectedly clutched his chest, crouched, and fell to his knees. Jack pushed himself off the ground and walked past his father and brother, who were confounded at what was happening. Max kneeled there at Jack's feet. It happened a second after there was a fleeting sound of something being shattered. Still on the ground, Max straightened his back, hands against that black heart of his.

"Then I'm God's messenger." Jack spoke in a broken, loathing voice, looking down on the man who had killed Thomas and tried to kill his family and Claire..

"YOOOUUU!" Max craned his neck up to look at Jack. Jack

opened his fist and let the dust of the broken stone filter through his fingers. Max's scream died together with him. The evil man dissolved into gray dust, just like that of the destroyed stone, and was diminished until there was nothing left of him. He was gone forever.

Jack exchanged a look with his brother and father. The rest were slowly coming to. Ivan looked up at Jack. "It's over," said Ivan in a dull tone. He didn't even seem relieved, just depressed.

Jack turned his head to the right where Claire lay, still motionless. But he still had hope in him. Somewhere… He ran to her and dropped to his knees beside her. She looked so peaceful. Mrs. Dawson was crying silently on her daughter's chest on one side, and Mr. Dawson crouched next to her on the other. Jack looked at him hopefully. He looked back at Jack and shook his head slowly, his eyes red and his face washed with tears. Jack breathed out and sat on the floor. The worst had happened, and all he could do was accept it. The only girl that he had ever loved was gone; life ahead seemed dull and bitter. Not even time could heal this wound…

***

Getting back home was the worst thing Jack had endured in his life. Especially when his family and the others had awoken to the terrible reality. Even more so when Vanessa opened her eyes to find her father, Thomas, dead and began wailing by his body. And Jack wished that he could wake up from this horrible nightmare, but there was none—this was all real. It was the worst reality that could exist, and now they had to live with the memory of it etched in their hearts for the rest of their lives…

***

Jessica knocked on the door to Jack's room, even though it was wide open. Jack did not answer. He was staring out the window up into the thick, gray clouds that covered the sky like a blanket. It was so dark and windy outside, yet there was not even as much as a drizzle. Jessica walked in together with Kyle.

"How are you holding up?" he asked sincerely as he patted Jack on the back and left his arm around his shoulder. Jack still didn't speak.

"Listen man, if you want to talk, you know your sister's right here."

Jack half smiled at Kyle's attempt to break the ice but continued gazing out the window.

"Jack, if there's anything you need, I shouldn't even be saying this but we're here for you. All of us. You know that," said Jessica.

"I know," he said.

"We'll wait outside for you." Jessica signaled her older brother to exit the room with her by looking at the door. Kyle gave his brother another firm tap on the back. "We love you, man."

Once they had left the room, Jack took the jacket belonging to the suit he was wearing and slid it on. He looked into the lean oval mirror, straightened his tie, and set the jacket firmly on his shoulders. For a moment he lingered before departing his bedroom and going outside to the driveway, where his father was waiting for him to drive to Claire and Thomas's funeral. His mother, Kyle, and Jessica were already seated in the car.

***

As though it knew what had happened and felt the same way as everyone else, the weather was glum. The emerald leaves on the weeping willows at Greensville cemetery were drooping, fluttering like scales in the pale daylight. The icy air stood still, the few birds sounding a fleeting *cheep* every now and then. Ben parked the car by the pavement, and the Sullivan family got out to pay their respects. Jack walked slowly, feeling every blade of grass as it crumpled under the soles of his shoes. The very sound of it was just loud enough to be heard with the whispers that hushed constantly. It felt to Jack as though the hum were piercing his ears, and he could barely abide it.

As he made his way toward the coffins, he caught Mr. Dawson's eye. Mr. Dawson nodded in recognition while hugging his crying wife, her face buried in his arms. Jack nodded once and came to a halt. He was standing in a circle of murmuring friends and family only ten feet or so from Claire's coffin. The second casket, beside Claire's, belonged to Thomas. Ivan and Vanessa were the only family of his that were still alive. They stood close to each other, their faces directed to the ground below.

Both pine boxes were polished and had a colorful wreath in the center with a sheet of white flowers covering the rest. It was a horrible sight. And then Jack looked at the spot where Claire was resting and had flashbacks.

"I had a great time tonight" Her voice was echoing in his head, and her face lingered before his eyes. Jack remembered dancing with her to her favorite song…her beautiful blue eyes…the first and only time they kissed…

Claire's face swam in his mind's eye, and Jack started crying for the first time since the tragedy. He cried silently and painfully, and then the parson spoke.

"We are all here today because of a terrible tragedy."

The wind began to swim softly through the leaves of the willows, the long branches of the one nearby flailing like a veil behind the decorated sarcophaguses.

"We lost a beloved daughter and friend, Claire Dawson…" A little muffled cry sounded at the mention of the girl's name. "An amazing young woman who has touched our lives in *(thud)* so many ways. I cannot even begin to describe *(thud, thud)* all the wonderful things that she has done…"

Jack looked up when he heard the sound for the second time. He was certain of it. He wiped his eyes and listened closely, ignoring the parson's voice in the background. And then he heard it again—*thud, thud*—and his heart was racing. He could feel it pounding like a pendulum, oscillating back and forth. Out of control. A rush of adrenalin flowed through him, and he acted without thinking. This was what he had to do, and he did not care what anyone might think or say or do.

Without further ado, Jack moved forward quickly, ignoring comments like, "What is he doing?" He bent over Claire's casket and shoved off all the decorative flowers, ignoring the gasps that people let out.

"Get him away from my daughter!" screeched Mrs. Dawson, and she cried even more hysterically than before. Meanwhile, George tried to pull Jack away, but Jack resisted and pushed him aside instead. Without hesitating, Jack lifted the top of the coffin, and the hinges creaked loudly.

Mrs. Dawson screamed again.

And then there was silence. Even the birds seemed to have hushed along with the wind. Jack reached in and pulled Claire out of the confinement of the wooden box. She was wearing a white dress and makeup, and her hair was fixed to hang neatly behind her back. Jack was holding her in his arms, and her arms were wrapped around his neck. She was crying heavily and hugged him so tightly he felt the breath pushed out of his lungs.

"My baby!" Mrs. Dawson stumbled and fainted; her husband was torn between reviving his wife and rushing to his daughter, who he, like everyone else, had thought was dead.

Jack brought Claire to her father and set her on her feet. "I love you," she whispered in his ear. Jack smiled at her fondly.

"Oh, Claire, I'm so happy you're here. I couldn't live without you," Mr. Dawson sobbed, and he and his daughter hurried to Mrs. Dawson and woke her up.

And that day had changed from sadness and misfortune to bewilderment and joy.

"It's a miracle!" cried a voice from the crowd.

And it truly was. Everybody's frowns had turned upside down, and tears of sadness had become those of contentment. But it was not a completely happy moment for two of the people in the cemetery that day. After approximately one minute, almost every single person in the place had turned their backs and headed home, all except the Dawsons.

There were only two people who were going in another direction.

"I'll be right there," Jack told Kyle, who was headed to the car.

"Ivan. Vanessa." Jack caught up with them at the willow close to the foot of Thomas's casket.

"You did a great thing there, Jack. You saved Claire's life." Ivan half smiled. "How did you know?"

"I heard."

"True love," said Ivan fondly.

"I didn't get a chance to speak to you after…" He paused and hesitated for a second "I'm sorry…about Thomas. He really was a good person. And even though I only knew him for two days, I'll never forget him. None of us will."

Vanessa smiled forlornly. "Thanks, he would've liked to know that."

"Thank you, Jack," Ivan said sincerely.

"So…are you going to be all right? I mean…"

"Jack," Ivan interrupted, "we are just as happy as you are that Claire is okay. It's a wonderful miracle. We just want to pay our respects to…my brother." When he said the last two words, tears sparkled in his eyes, and Vanessa wiped her face with her sleeve.

"I'll leave you to it." Jack smiled faintly and turned, and as he walked past the closed casket he said softly, "Goodbye Thomas."

"I'll always watch over you, little brother." Ivan coughed with watery eyes.

"I didn't get a chance to tell you this lately, but…" Vanessa choked. "I love you, Dad." She turned to her uncle and sobbed heavily into his jacket.

Ivan opened the door for his niece and then climbed into the driver's seat. The engine moaned as they drove away, the last ones to leave the cemetery.

ONE MONTH LATER...

"Happy birthday to you,
Happy birthday to you,
Happy birthday, dear Claire
Happy birthday to you."

Claps and whistles erupted in the Dawsons' crowded lounge as the frosted cake was put on the table by a proud Mrs. Dawson, her chest puffed up like an ostrich as she pranced. "Make a wish!" she told her daughter excitedly.

"Okay!" Claire bent over the cake, hesitated, and then blew out the eighteen small candles on the large, round cake. Cheers and claps erupted once again, friends and family celebrating cheerfully.

A few people from the crowd pushed their way to the birthday girl.

"Wow, thanks you guys, you really didn't have to."

"Of course we did!" said Allison shrilly.

"It's your birthday, isn't it?" said Richard happily.

Next in line was Ivan. "He's right, you know. Most of these people are just here to give you presents. I'm sure you hardly know half these people." He handed her an envelope.

"Thank you so much. It's good to see you," she said grinning. "Hey, Vanessa!"

She'd just popped out from behind her uncle. Ivan went to stand by the window. "Happy birthday!" she said gleefully. They hugged each other.

"Hi, girls." Jack had just made his way through the cluster of people.

"Oh, he's got a gift." Vanessa raised her eyebrows. "I'll go get us something to drink." She and Claire both giggled.

"What was that?" asked Jack when she left.

"Nothing. Just girl stuff." Claire said. "Oh, check this out!"

Claire opened her hand, and it glowed with white-blue electric sparks. "I've been practicing."

That was why Claire had somehow survived Max's attack that night in *Il L'Arco*. She had an ability of her own brewing within that not even she knew about.

"Impressive! This…" Jack handed her a slim rectangular jewelry box, "…is for you."

"Wow!" exclaimed Claire when she saw the silver necklace inside. "It's beautiful."

"Here, let me put it on for you." Jack slipped the necklace under her hair and clipped it at the back of her neck. For a moment, they looked into each other's eyes and kissed.

Vanessa came back with a bottle of Coke and three disposable cups fit into one another.

"Oh, c'mon, Jack. Don't feel awkward."

Jack gave her a sardonic smile.

The three resumed conversation as the party went on, music playing loudly in the background.

Ivan had poured himself a cup of soda and was standing by

the window, staring through the wet glass. Thinking about his brother…

Outside, the rain poured heavily, showering the grass and plants below. Leaves fell from the trees, plummeting to the ground. The branches of the old willow swayed gracefully in the wind like vines above the white tombstone that read: *Thomas Redford, beloved father, husband, and brother. 1958–2017.*

In an instant, the falling rain changed its course and flew in every direction as the grave exploded. Shards of pearl-white marble scattered all around. Large misshapen pieces of pine wood fell to the ground, covered in flames. The bits of fire flickered, trying to remain alight as the rain slowly fought to put them out. Burned splinters settled quickly on the ground below. A few of the weeping willow's branches had been charred, too.

Now, where there had been a grave was a crater shaped roughly like a rectangle. From within, swathed in ragged black and white material, emerged an arm. It perched itself on the wet earth, gripping tightly, and its master hoisted himself out.

Thomas struggled onto his back, leaning on his elbows, head held up and looking around, astounded, breathing rapidly in complete shock, not knowing how he could still be alive.

21859499R00094

Printed in Poland
by Amazon Fulfillment
Poland Sp. z o.o., Wrocław